Rival Hearts

Other books in the Quilts of Love Series

RIVAL HEARTS

Quilts of Love Series

Tara Randel

Abingdon fiction™
a novel approach to faith

Nashville

Rival Hearts

Copyright © 2014 by Tara Spicer

ISBN-13: 978-1-4267-7346-4

Published by Abingdon Press, P.O. Box 801, Nashville, TN 37202

www.abingdonpress.com

Published in association with the Steve Laube Agency

All rights reserved.

The persons and events portrayed in this work of fiction
are the creations of the author, and any resemblance
to persons living or dead is purely coincidental.

Library of Congress Cataloging-in-Publication Data

Randel, Tara.
 Rival hearts / Tara Randel.
     pages cm. — (Quilts of Love series)
 ISBN 978-1-4267-7346-4 (soft back, adhesive perfect binding : alk. paper) 1. Journalists—Fiction.
2. Journalism—Competitions—Fiction. 3. Quilting—Fiction. 4. Journalism, Outdoor—Fiction.
I. Title.
 PS3618.A64R58 2014
 813'.6—dc23

                                                                          2013046901

Printed in the United States of America

1 2 3 4 5 6 7 8 9 10 / 19 18 17 16 15 14

Dedication

To my family and friends at River of Praise Church. You are a wonderful group of people. I'm honored to serve God with you.

Acknowledgments

To my agent, Tamela Hancock Murray. From the first time we spoke, I knew we would work well together. I appreciate your patience as we got things rolling. I'm excited to see what we will do together in the future. Thanks, from the bottom of my heart.

To Pastor John and Pam Schneider. Words can't express how much I value your friendship. Thank you for your shoulders to cry on and for listening to Randy and me make sense of life after Megan. You are both so faithful. May God richly bless you both.

1

Molly Henderson forced herself to remain still, even though every fiber in her being wanted to scoot to the end of the chair and rattle off at least twenty questions that came to mind. "A challenge?"

Her boss, imposing as he sat in his leather chair behind an enormous mahogany desk, steepled fingers under his chin. Self-satisfaction curved his lips. "Let's call it a little in-house competition between you and Ben. The winner will be editor-in-chief of my new magazine, *American Legend*."

Pushing her glasses higher on her nose, Molly's gaze darted to Ben Weaver, the man who had just gone from colleague to competitor. His veiled expression showed no emotion. Was he as surprised as she? Of all the topics this meeting could have entailed, informing them of a competition hadn't been one of them.

She'd been surprised by the impromptu call to the boss's office. Equally surprised when she found Ben waiting to attend the same meeting. What a way to start her Wednesday morning.

"My plan is unusual, I know. Both of you are qualified for the position and would do an excellent job." He shrugged. "I decided to put my own spin on the promotion process."

Putting his own spin on things had made Blake Masterson a very successful publisher. His unorthodox style of management set him apart in the publishing world, but somehow it worked for him. Mid-fifties, self-made, and very popular in the Tampa Bay area for his publicity stunts. The stunts captivated the public, but always brought notice to charitable organizations and needs in the community. The man had a savvy mind and knew how to use it to keep his company in the limelight.

"As you know, Master's Publishing is ready to expand with a new magazine. I need people focused for the long haul to get the magazine up and running and to handle day-to-day operations afterward. You have both proven valuable in your current editorial roles and I want to see where this challenge will take you."

Molly bit back a sigh. She'd been with Master's Publishing for eight years now, four as senior editor and writer for *Quilter's Heart Magazine*. She loved working for the company, but steered clear of Mr. Masterson's publicity stunts. She had seniority; her longevity alone should give her first shot at the position. But a competition involving her? Honestly, she'd never been very good at any endeavor outside her comfort zone, which consisted of working behind the scenes or immersing herself in a quilting project. Given the determined look on her boss's face, his grand plan would definitely be uncomfortable for her.

But not for her soon-to-be rival.

She sneaked another peek at Ben. Tall, built, tan, and extremely masculine. Not to mention the most soulful brown eyes she'd ever seen. Yes, the man was handsome. But his ego? Another story all together.

They'd rubbed each other the wrong way since the first day he stormed into Master's Publishing six months ago to take over as senior editor and head writer of *Outdoor Adventures Magazine*. He'd smiled his confident smile and acted like he owned the place. He assured Mr. Masterson his former freelance writing and television experience would increase circulation of his magazine and far outsell all the other magazines published by Master's, including "the little quilting magazine," as he referred to Molly's magazine. He made friends with all the staff, frequently took over meetings, and whenever she tried to make suggestions, he smiled down at her, not taking her seriously. She never let on how much he bugged her, but, boy, did he bug her. And now a competition? Ben would relish any out-of-the-box trial thrown his way. This was so unfair.

"I've been very impressed with both of you. Our sales have increased due to both your efforts and we've already made a presence with our digital editions.

"Ben, before you took on *Outdoor Adventures*, I was ready to pull the brand, but the articles are entertaining and well-written. The results have increased the circulation and advertising revenue. Of course, your past foray into the cable television show *Extreme Survivors* helped ramp up circulation. After watching you on TV, I jumped at the chance to lure you onboard. Nothing like having a mini-celebrity on staff."

Yes, Molly knew that part, since everyone in the office talked about him.

Mr. Masterson grinned, as if Ben's fame would benefit him. "I allowed you to fulfill your prior commitments when you first took the job, but since the traveling has wound down, we're happy to have you in the office full-time."

Some people, Molly thought.

"I have to give credit to Charlie," Ben said as he leaned back in his chair. "He kept the magazine going while I finished up my schedule."

"Always good to have a competent assistant, especially one who knows what readers want. Since you've shown your dedication, I thought you might want a shot at the new position."

"Yes sir, I would," he said, his smile dazzling.

"Good. Good." Mr. Masterson turned to Molly.

"Molly, you've been here since you started as an intern. When you came up with the idea for a quilting magazine, I have to say I wasn't convinced the market could sustain it. But you kept after me and proved me wrong. Who knew crafts were so popular? You've built a readership and the numbers keep growing, but you haven't quite gotten to the place where readers connect you with Master's Publishing.

"Your monthly Dear Reader column is great but it's time to take your relationship with your readers to the next level. I know you're working on a special project to connect with readers, but let's up the ante. Get them behind you."

Which Ben, with his high profile in the extreme sports world, had already done in just six months.

"Even though both magazines are regional, as editors, I'm sure you'd like to work on a bigger project like *American Legend*. You both have a knack for finding in-depth human-interest stories to touch your particular readers. Just the type of content I want for my new magazine. Stories featuring ordinary people doing extraordinary things in their lives—not expecting accolades—just doing what comes naturally. I want stories of derring-do, faith-based stories, tearjerkers whenever possible. You'll be given a chance to shine as an editor as well as moving up in the company."

Rumors had infiltrated the office for weeks now that Mr. Masterson had something in the works. Speculation about the new magazine ran the gamut from parenting advice, to the auto industry, even a new comic book division. With Mr. Masterson's love for giving back to the community, *American Legend* was a perfect choice for his reputation. And while Molly appreciated the idea, she still had questions.

"Could you be more specific?" she asked, still unsure about her part in this latest development. "About the challenge?"

With pen and paper in hand to jot down notes perhaps affecting her future with the publisher, she waited patiently. She loved being an editor, loved her magazine. But a promotion? Who wouldn't jump at the chance?

"Out of all our inventory of magazines, both of yours are the most popular. Top sellers, actually. And polar opposites. So I thought, why not have my two top editors switch places? Molly, you belong to a quilting group, right? The one you've mentioned in your column?"

"Right."

Mr. Masterson turned to Ben. "You will join Molly's quilting group. Let's find out if those outdoor skills of yours translate into sewing and producing a well-made finished product."

"Quilting?" Ben raised a questioning eyebrow.

Oh, her friends would love this. Her boss had no idea of the dynamics in an all-female gathering. Ben might be used to his rough-and-tumble world, where strength and experience with Mother Nature gave him the upper hand in the wilderness. Spending an hour with suburban moms who talked about love, life, kids, what to make for dinner, and what their husbands were in trouble for, might send him screaming into the sunset. She'd seen the caged look on many faces of men forced to spend too much together time in a room with chatty women. Ben didn't know it yet, but he'd just signed up for an adventure very few men could withstand and survive to tell the tale.

"Right now you're working on the next issue of *Outdoor Adventures*, which features . . ." Mr. Masterson glanced down at his notes. "Kayaking?"

"Yes."

"Perfect. Molly—"

Please, please, please, not sports. No physical activities. Anything but the outdoors. Her pulse rate elevated and she held her breath while she braced herself.

"—we'll get you hooked up with a local kayaking event. Since Ben already has some activities lined up for the next issue, here's a perfect opportunity to show me what you're made of."

"Kayaking?" Molly croaked, echoing Ben's earlier response to his challenge.

"Afterward, we'll showcase your individual journeys in your magazines." Mr. Masterson shot them a teasing wink. "I do love publicity. And friendly competition."

Molly gripped her pen. Friendly? More like a battle of the sexes if you asked her. One she doubted Ben would make easy. He took on a challenge the way an explorer took on the jungle, divide and conquer. No way could she kayak a few feet from shore, let alone with some major activity cooked up by Ben. She doubted she could get in the thing without tipping over.

"You'll each have four weeks to complete your tasks. At the end of the month, I'll review your progress and name the new editor-in-chief. Any questions?"

Ben spoke up first. "Yes, sir. Where will my new office be located?"

"Your office?" Molly sputtered.

He smiled at her. "Yes. My office."

"Don't you mean *my* new office space?" she countered.

Mr. Masterson stood. "Both of you follow me."

He led them down the hallway from his office. All the offices on this floor were for upper management, while one story down housed the other departments, including her office and Ben's. Once they reached their destination, Masterson stood to the side as he opened the door with a grand flourish. Ben, his eyes bright with success, motioned for Molly to enter ahead of him. The more confident he appeared, the more steamed she became. No way would she let him win.

The vacant office had more square feet than both Molly and Ben's current offices combined. Wide windows overlooked downtown Tampa, offering a glimpse of the vast city spread out before them. Bright sunlight glinted off Tampa Bay, where boats zig-zagged across clear azure water. From a closer view, eleven stories below, cars moved in a steady stream of traffic alongside a city park dotted with benches located under palm trees and plenty of grassy area before ending at the banks of the Hillsborough River.

Standing before the windows, Molly savored the sunshine and forced herself to calm down. Her inside office had no windows while Ben had managed to procure an outer office with one window. What she wouldn't give for this spectacular view every day.

Ben might be Mr. Masterson's bright, shining star, but Molly had grown tired of working her tail off with little reward. As much as she loved *Quilter's Heart*, lately she'd been antsy. Ready for a change. A challenge would shake up her life, hopefully in a good way. And the best outcome? To beat out Ben for the job.

She turned just in time to see Ben place his briefcase on the empty desk, remove a clear plastic cube with a baseball inside, and set it on the smooth surface. His gaze met hers, telling her with no words necessary he'd marked the place as his. She bit back a retort because their boss hovered in the doorway, but she vowed to make him eat those unspoken words.

"Before you two plan your individual battle strategies, I suggest you return to your desks and figure out the logistics of the challenge." Mr. Masterson motioned for them to exit the office. "I'll stay in the loop to see how you're both progressing. I may want to tweak things a bit as the competition heats up."

Bad enough she had to compete, but knowing Mr. Masterson might throw in a game changer somewhere along the line? Great. Just great.

Being dismissed, Molly walked on shaky legs, allowing Ben to precede her. He couldn't know how her boss's grand scheme, or Ben's confidence in assuming he'd won the challenge before it had started, rattled her. Never had she imagined she'd have to prove herself in such an unusual way. She'd been a loyal employee for years. Had doubled the circulation of her magazine in her time as editor. Shouldn't her work ethic have merit in her boss's decision?

She joined Ben by the elevator, tugging the lapels of her jacket over her blouse. Her mind ran in so many different directions, she couldn't focus on any one thought. She glanced up to watch the progress of the elevator as numbers lit up above the door, trying to ignore the hunky man who now worked against her. Ben hadn't said much after the question in Mr. Masterson's office and the silence grated on her sensitive nerves. Finally, he turned her way.

"Do you have anything planned right now?"

"Just heading back to my office."

"Mind if I tag along? We can discuss the challenge details."

Details. Right. If only she could ignore him like she wanted to. Suspicious, she asked, "Why my office?"

He chuckled. "Either will do. I thought you might be more comfortable hammering out the details on your own turf."

Oh, sure. Now he decides to be accommodating, unlike his confident assumption he'd be moving into the upstairs office. "Fine."

The elevator doors parted and Ben nodded for her to board first. He entered, pressed the button for their floor and the doors slid shut, followed by a jerk of movement.

Molly stared at her fuzzy reflection in the metal doors. Why did these things always feel so small? And why did Ben have to stand so close? His shoulder brushed hers, but she held her ground. No way would she shy away from him.

Instead, she tapped her foot to the canned music playing some oldie but goodie.

"Something wrong?" he asked.

"No. Just enjoying the music."

"You're off beat."

She stopped. Stood stiffly. "Guess we all can't be good at everything."

He chuckled again.

The close confines made her antsy. When the doors opened, she hoofed it to her office. Once inside, she relaxed. Her turf indeed.

To one side, a comfy armchair and end table neatly displayed the most recent issues of *Quilter's Heart* magazine. Along the opposite wall, a long table held a sewing caddy with her quilting supplies and an assortment of folded fabric on top. Fresh potpourri scented the air. As she closed the door, the busy sounds from the office diminished. She smoothed her skirt and took a seat behind her desk, adjusting the desk calendar containing daily Scriptures.

Her domain. Her little place in the vast world of publishing. Small as it might be, everything was neat and tidy, in its place, just the way she liked it.

Until Ben walked in and stirred up her senses with a megadose of testosterone.

Why did she let him get to her? He'd grabbed her attention right from the first day they'd met, thinking how fun it would be to work with a handsome, world-traveling guy. Until he opened his mouth and ticked her off. Since then she'd done her best to ignore him, but right now, his very male presence in her very female office had her hormones in an uproar.

Hiding her reaction from Ben, she pulled her best business face and motioned for him to take a seat in the chair before her desk.

His large hand pulled the chair back a few inches to make room for his long legs. Today he wore a pastel blue button-down shirt with navy slacks and loafers. Almost like he knew to dress up for the meeting, since he usually wore more casual, athletic clothes to the office. But he didn't know about the meeting, so, of course, he couldn't have planned his wardrobe.

And did he have to smell so good? His sandalwood cologne had distracted her from the moment she took a seat next to him in Mr. Masterson's office, just as it did now.

Stop.

With a flick of her hand, she centered her pen and pad on the desktop before brushing her hair from her shoulder, waiting for him to speak.

"So what do you think about Masterson's idea?" he asked, as he lowered himself into the chair.

"I think it's crazy."

He waved a hand. "Yeah. I know Masterson likes his stunts, but even I have to admit the idea is a little out there. He doesn't usually involve his employees."

"Guess we're his guinea pigs."

Ben's eyes flashed humor. "You up for a little challenge?"

What did he mean? He didn't think she could handle an out-door challenge? She didn't miss the way his gaze took in her wavy blonde hair, brown-framed glasses and body curves. Okay, her glasses might present a functional problem and she could shed a few pounds, but those minor obstacles didn't mean she couldn't complete the challenge.

"I'm as up to it as you are," she asserted, a little miffed and on the offensive. "I want the job."

"So do I."

"Do you plan on sticking around to see the outcome?"

"What do you mean?"

"It isn't a secret you love to travel. What's different now?"

He took a moment to answer. Sorrow flashed across his strong features, gone just as quickly as it came. "I have my reasons."

"Ben, I've been here a long time. I'm the face of stability. Can you make the same assertion?"

"You don't know what I bring to the table."

"Exactly. Does anyone?"

His eyes narrowed, humor gone.

"Wouldn't it be easier for all involved for you to step back and let me, the person with seniority, take the position?"

16

"Yes. Very easy. But I don't like easy." His steady gaze met hers. "We're competitors."

His predatory smile sent goose bumps over her skin. She recognized the look, had seen it right before he jumped off a cliff into churning water or let out a yell as a parasail took him high above the ocean. Yeah, she watched television, too.

"Look, Ben, I may not seem like an outdoorsy kind of girl, but I can be pretty single-minded when I want something."

"Yeah?" He chuckled. "No offense, but when was the last time you spent any time outdoors?"

"And I could ask, when have you ever sewn anything?"

His gaze focused on the wall behind her head as he thought. "About a year ago. We were camped in the middle of nowhere in the Australian outback. The canvas tent ripped in a freaky wind storm and I had to repair it with some spare fishing line."

Of course he did.

"Not the same as stitching with a fine needle and thread on much more delicate fabric."

He shrugged. "I'll adapt."

Wouldn't he just.

Well, so would she. She hadn't grown up with overprotective parents not to have the backbone to reach deep down and go after the editor-in-chief position. Hadn't she been proving herself all her life? It seemed like it, especially when her accomplishments were always secondary compared to a brother who excelled at everything he did.

Her gaze settled on Ben. Not much different from now.

For all her bravado, she'd worry about the actual challenge itself later. After she Googled kayaking and figured out what she'd been forced into. First, she needed to make Ben believe he had something to worry about.

Before she had a chance, he stood, as if ready to leave, when he noticed her partially completed quilt top draped over the quilt rack in the corner. He walked over. "It looks like a jigsaw puzzle."

She grinned. He wasn't far off in his assessment. "I can see why you'd think so. There aren't enough pieces stitched together yet to make the pattern discernible."

"So what's it going to be?"

"The pattern is called Hearts Entwined." She grabbed a picture from her desk and handed it to him. The pattern, so romantic in her mind, would show even more beautifully when she finished the piece.

On a white background, separate geometric shapes of triangles, squares and diamonds in dark red came together to form a heart. The same shapes in pale pink formed another heart.

"If you look at the colored fabric, you'll see once the pieces are stitched together, it resembles two hearts inside each other, the red one right side up, the pink one upside down. With the contrasting colors, it looks like hearts entwined."

A narrow, deep red border surrounded the heart shapes, making them stand out. The piece would be finished off with a wide white border with matching red and pink squares in the four corners. She hadn't yet picked out a fabric for the backing, but she'd get to it soon.

He tilted his head. "Yeah, I can see. Clever."

She couldn't resist a smile. Most guys would have just agreed to placate her, not taking a good look at the intricate pattern to see the design. Knowing how Ben operated, getting down to the nitty-gritty of most things, she shouldn't be surprised by his interest.

"Are you working on this?"

Joining him, Molly ran her fingers over the soft material. "Yes. It's a special project I came up with for the next *Quilter's Heart* issue."

"How so?"

"Every year I make a quilt and auction it off at the local Charity Expo held in the beginning of May. I got an idea to have my readers send in a piece of fabric holding emotional significance to them, along with the story to go with it. Once the quilt is finished, I'll showcase the finished piece and the stories from my readers in *Quilter's Heart*. This way they get to be part of the quilting experience. Then, it'll be auctioned at the Expo."

He looked at the fabric swatches on the worktable. "Looks like a lot of work left. It's already the beginning of April."

"I'll finish," she assured him. Or herself, anyway. With everything going on in her life lately and the challenge thrown into the mix, she would indeed cut it close.

After putting out a reader all-call for fabric six months ago, material had trickled in. She thought her idea might be a bust and worried she'd made a colossal mistake. Once the deadline approached, however, a deluge of fabric arrived at the office. With more than enough to complete the project, Molly had begun cutting out the pattern and started stitching the pieces together by hand. Then, two weeks ago, she'd had to stop.

An organization she volunteered for, Second Chances, faced a disaster. A kitchen fire had caused major damage in the facility where women who were victims of domestic abuse trained for jobs. Thankfully, the shelter, which housed women who had eluded their abusive partners before transitioning their lives, had escaped the fire. Between the burned-out kitchen and smoke damage, Molly and others had been working at the center to move what they could to another donated location and keep the programs going during construction to get the center back to normal. She just now had time in her schedule to get back to the quilting project.

"It's a nice idea." His deep, brown eyes focused on her. "So will I be working on this quilt?"

Horrified, Molly's eyes widened. "No way."

"No need to get touchy."

"You'll be working on whatever my group is sewing."

He glanced at the quilt-in-progress and frowned.

"Thinking sewing a tent might be a piece of cake, right now?"

"I'm thinking our boss is a very shrewd man. Admit it. We've both got a big learning curve ahead of us."

"Maybe."

"Most definitely." Ben caught her gaze. "I don't suppose your quilting group will be easy on me?"

"Not any easier than me getting the hang of kayaking." She held back a sigh. "With the Expo next month, I've got to get busy."

He turned back to the quilt top. "You'll finish in a month?"

She masked the concern in her voice. "I'll get it done." Worried or not, she wouldn't let Ben see any weakness.

"I'll be the first to admit making a quilt looks pretty complicated, but when was the last time you participated in any sporting activity?"

"It's been a while."

"Right." The grin again. "So I have a proposition."

She regarded him with suspicion. "Which is?"

"How about I give you a head start? Then you can begin getting used to the kayak so when you have to succeed in your part of the challenge, you don't die on me."

Her cheeks grew hot. "First of all, I won't die. And second, I don't need your help."

"The boss said we can figure out the details between us." He eyed her from head to toe again. "I can afford to help you out."

Okay, his comment had her steamed. "How generous of you," she snapped.

"I'm a generous kind of guy."

"As much as I appreciate your offer," she said as she opened the door to see him out, "I'm going to decline. Once you get started quilting, you'll be wishing *I* gave *you* a head start."

He might *think* he had the advantage, but with his attitude, she'd show him her spunky side. If anything in her life made her want to step it up and prove she could master the challenge, his words sealed the deal.

Ben bit back a chuckle. Miss Molly thought she had it under control. He'd let her keep thinking she had a shot, right up until the boss appointed him editor-in-chief.

He sauntered back to his office. Who knew Molly had a backbone? A pretty solid one from what he could see. By her refusal of a head start, he had no doubt she wanted the new position as much as he did and would work hard to win. He'd never seen her assertive side before. Even though he hadn't had the opportunity to work with her on any projects, he had seen her around the office. And most of those times she'd been quiet, busy with her tasks, but he'd taken notice of her. Unassuming, but she'd caught his eye. Now he had the chance to find out more about the real Molly.

Ever since returning to Tampa, he hadn't yet renewed any old friendships or made new ones, in or out of the office. After a cycling accident in France eight months ago, he'd decided to step back from the television show. His injuries—massively scraped-up arms and legs along with a sprained wrist and concussion—were not life-threatening but were enough to keep him on the sidelines for a few weeks when his recuperation didn't fit into the filming schedule. When the camera crew moved on to the next location, Ben found himself abandoned in a foreign country. Alone. He hadn't liked it one bit.

During the downtime, he had an epiphany. He wanted a change in his normally hectic life. His parents had loved to travel, taking him on grand vacations from Alaska to Fiji from the time he could walk. They were the ones who encouraged him to pursue his dreams. After their deaths, he'd still traveled, but stayed away from Tampa and the memories of a happy childhood swimming and boating in Florida waters. By refusing to settle down, he'd missed out on having a support system. Friends he could call on in an emergency. It couldn't have been any clearer than while he recuperated in France.

Traveling had become old hat, losing its appeal and challenge with no one to share it with. He was thirty-five, with no permanent home. No people in his life to depend on. Much as he tried to make it work, his television crew couldn't take the place of family. A high-profile position for the new magazine would allow him to put down roots. Reconnect with childhood friends he saw too infrequently. Instead of running, he wanted to come home. A sense of permanence. Miss Molly was not going to keep him from getting what he longed for.

"Hey, Ben. Got a minute?"

Charlie, Ben's assistant editor came up beside him, a folder in his pudgy hands. Slightly overweight, sporting glasses and thinning hair, he didn't resemble an athletic type of guy, but he sure knew the business of sports and publishing. He could recite statistics from football, baseball, or hockey in his sleep.

"Sure. What's up?"

"I've been going over scheduling for the next issue," Charlie said as he followed Ben into the office. "I've confirmed a kayak excursion for this month. I can assign a writer who will cover the story and interview the participants."

He couldn't have asked for more perfect timing. "You don't need to find a writer."

"What are you talking about?"

"I have someone lined up."

Charlie waited a beat before asking, "Who?"

"Molly."

"Molly." Charlie's round face scrunched up in confusion. "You mean quilting Molly?"

"She's the one."

"You want to run that by me again?"

He explained the challenge Masterson has just issued.

"So, Molly will be taking up kayaking." Charlie blinked. "I just can't see it."

Neither could Ben, but who was he to argue? It was evident from the boxy jackets Molly wore to hide her curves—she didn't exercise much. It didn't matter—he liked her look. Her wavy, shoulder-length hair and the ever-present glasses covering intelligent blue eyes gave her a studious air he found attractive. She had a passion for quilting, a quick mind and, as he'd learned today, an even quicker tongue. But at the same time, her apparent lack of athletic ability gave him an advantage. If she trained hard enough, she might be able to pull it off. But he doubted it. In fact, he depended on it.

"And you have to take up quilting?" Charlie asked.

"Yep."

While Molly's office held all sorts of quilting doodads, sporting equipment littered Ben's. A bow and arrow stood in one corner, camping essentials he hadn't had a chance to sort through since returning to Tampa dumped in another. Paperwork piled up on his desk. Paperwork he'd intended to get to before the call to the morning's meeting with Masterson.

Sunlight streamed through the window. Even though his office was tiny, Ben couldn't help feeling a little guilty that he managed to get space with natural lighting while Molly's work space resembled an oversized cubicle. No wonder she wanted the big office upstairs. And from the way her eyes had narrowed when he placed his prized baseball on the empty desk, he may have stirred up more in Molly than he bargained for.

Taking a few more minutes to give Charlie more details on the challenge, he saw doubt in his assistant's eyes.

"Do you even know how to sew?" Charlie asked, still puzzled by Ben's part of the challenge.

"I'll figure it out. How hard can it be?"

"It's sewing," Charlie stated, as if Ben were dense.

"Yeah. So?"

"I don't know any guys who sew."

"You will now."

"Okay, so what if you win? What happens then?"

"Not if. When," Ben told him. "If you play your cards right, buddy, you might end up in this office."

Charlie glanced around the room, a sly grin curving his lips. "Think I'll get promoted?"

"Why not? You've been working with *Outdoor Adventures* long enough to take over my job."

"I'm liking this challenge more and more."

"Don't get ahead of yourself. I have to win first."

Charlie tossed the file on Ben's desk. "With you in the driver's seat, all I have to do is sit back and enjoy the ride."

2

A knock on the door startled Molly out of her concentration as she hovered over the computer keyboard.

"Sorry to bother you," Taylor, her assistant editor, said as she entered the office. She'd been with Molly for two years and they worked well together. With long, straight brunette hair, hazel eyes, and a trim physique, she resembled the proverbial girl next door. "I have news."

"So do I."

Taylor's brows shot up. "Oh, please. You're always the last one in the office to have juicy news."

"Today things change around here."

"Nope. I know about the challenge."

Exasperated, Molly flopped back in her chair. "I just found out."

"Not really. It's been at least an hour."

Molly glanced at her watch. She'd spent the last hour scouring the Internet on everything kayak-related, when she could have made better use of her time by working. "You got me."

Taylor leaned against Molly's desk. "Here's the scoop. We know you and Ben are going against each other for the editor-in-chief position of the new magazine Master's Publishing is planning to launch. I want details later, but for now, let's stay on track. You deserve the promotion, of course, but we decided to make it an office-wide wager."

"We? Who are *we*? And what is the wager for?"

"The office staff. Girls vs. guys. I got voted leader of Team Molly."

Molly let out a groan. "Like I need the additional pressure."

"You thrive under pressure."

"Since when?"

"Since always."

Hmm. Did she? She'd never thought so.

"I've seen you down to the wire on a deadline and you never break a sweat."

"Well, I'm about to start sweating." Molly grimaced. "Kayaking? I am so not an outdoor girl."

"You're about to become one. All the ladies in the office have your back."

"Thanks. It's nice to—"

"Besides," Taylor rushed on, "you don't expect Ben to win, do you?"

"He says he has sewing experience."

Taylor looked at her like she'd lost her mind. "Nature Boy? Please. His sewing experience amounts to lacing up his boots."

"Nature Boy?"

"Yeah. It's what we call him around the office."

"Nature Boy. I like it." Molly's grin turned to a frown. "Why didn't I know he has a nickname?"

"Because you're so busy, you miss a lot of stuff."

"Like what?"

"Like Rosie got her fiancé to set a wedding date and Bob's Lab had puppies."

How had she missed all the office gossip? She needed to spend more time with her coworkers. "Boy, I am off. But not about Ben."

"You don't think a guy who is used to high-adrenaline action is going to be able to sit for hours at a time with a needle in his big, calloused hands, do you? He'll go batty the first day."

"I thought so too, but he's very determined."

"So are we."

We. Again, no pressure.

"Look," Taylor reasoned. "You've worked here for years. You know the ins and outs of Master's Publishing. And with you going up against the good old boys' club, what better way to pave the way for the rest of the women in the office? Can Ben do the same?"

"He's a good editor, Taylor. Even if we wish otherwise."

"True. Oh, and just so you know, Charlie is heading up the guy's cheering section."

Molly wrinkled her nose. "You'll have your work cut out for you."

"Yeah, he's not the nicest guy around, but I still say you're going to win."

Thinking back on the events of the day, the meeting with Mr. Masterson and then hashing out the details with Ben, Molly needed Taylor to bounce ideas off of. Who else in the office could she confide in? Only Taylor.

"So, Ben and I had a sit-down about our parts in the challenge. He's sure he has the job and we haven't even started yet." She told Taylor about the scene in the office upstairs.

"Typical Ben."

"About the office, yes. But Ben's so confident he'll win, he offered to give me a head start."

Taylor punched her fist in the air. "Yes."

"Don't get all excited. I refused."

"Why?"

"It didn't seem right. In an odd way, we're in it together."

"That's your problem," Taylor informed her. "You're so black and white."

"It's fair."

"Yeah, if you win."

Molly took off her glasses and rubbed her weary eyes. "I have no idea where to start."

Taylor thought about it for a moment. "Get your hunky brother to help you while he's in town."

She hadn't thought of him. Paul was on leave from the Marines, recovering from surgery for a shoulder injury sustained during a training exercise.

"I don't know."

"He's in shape and knows a thing or two about fitness. And he's family. Call him."

She'd spent the better part of her life not expecting her family's help. She doubted she could start now. "I don't want to bother him. Although, he's probably bored to tears resting at my parents' house. He and downtime don't go well together."

Taylor pointed to the phone on Molly's desk. "Won't know until you ask."

"True." Stalling, Molly glanced at the folder Taylor had laid on her desk. "Did you finish cataloguing the fabric samples for the Hearts Entwined quilt?"

"Yes. I took a picture of each piece and attached it to the letter so you know who sent it and the story behind the fabric."

"Did any stories stand out to you?"

"Yes. I typed up an additional list of candidates. It's in the folder."

"Great. I made a list of my favorites as well. We'll go over them together next week."

"I've got some other work to catch up on." Concern etched Taylor's face. She might be Molly's assistant, but they were also friends. "Are you going to be okay?"

Molly waved a hand. "Once I get my mind wrapped around the fact I have to compete in an outdoor activity."

"You can do anything you put your mind to, Molly."

She didn't have much choice. If she wanted the promotion, which she did, she'd have to dig deep and impress Mr. Masterson. No matter how much Ben grated on her nerves, she would learn to kayak. For the women in the office, to prove Ben wrong, and most importantly, to prove to herself she was worthy enough to get what she wanted. "With you rooting for me, how can I fail?"

"That's the attitude." Taylor walked to the door then paused, turning a mischievous smile on Molly. "Call your brother. If you don't, I will."

"You'll use any excuse to talk to him, won't you?"

"Yes, ma'am." With a wink, Taylor turned on her heel and marched out the door.

As her assistant left the office, Molly stared at the phone, torn. With the eight-year age difference between them, they weren't close. He'd always excelled at sports, breezed through high school with the popular crowd, unlike her, and after joining the Marines, moved up the ranks. He'd enlisted years ago, been deployed twice, and returned home for holidays when he could make it or was in the country. Back home a couple of days now, she had yet to visit him.

Guilt played on the edges of her mind. What kind of sister was she not to visit her injured brother? The kind of baby sister who always took second place in the hearts of her parents. She'd been a surprise late-in-life child. From an early age she'd battled numerous allergies, which left her odd man out, so unlike her active brother. She'd grown up in his enormous shadow. After a while, she didn't bother trying to impress parents with whom she felt invisible. Her childhood woes were not Paul's fault, but he probably hadn't even realized what was going on in her life back then. Still, she should call him and ask for help. What's the worst he could do, say no?

She took a breath and picked up the receiver with one hand while pressing the numbers with the other.

"Hey, little Sis. What's up?"

"I'm sorry I haven't made it over to Mom and Dad's to see you. My life has been chaotic lately."

"Hey, I figured my very responsible sister would show up at some point."

"How are you doing?"

"Other than stir-crazy?"

She laughed, picturing her six-foot-tall brother itching to get outside. Knowing their mother, she'd keep an eagle eye on Paul as he recuperated, which also wouldn't sit well.

"I'll be by later. I want to talk to you about something at work."

"Sounds intriguing."

"Well, I wouldn't go that far, but I need to ask a favor."

She took a moment to brace herself and noted the silence at the other end of the line.

"What is it?" His voice deepened. "Some guy giving you trouble?"

Yes, but not in the way her brother meant. And she wasn't about to give him ammo to set his sights on Ben.

"It's a work thing, kind of involved, but it's sports-related."

"Did you just say sports?"

She chuckled. "I know, right? I'll fill you in when I come over tonight."

"Not going anywhere."

She hung up, optimistic. If she could convince Paul to train her, she might have a level playing field against Ben. At this point, she'd take any lead she could get.

Rising from her chair, she walked to her worktable. With about three-quarters of the quilt top completed, she might be safe with the timeline, if she didn't drop the ball. Of all the story ideas she'd come up with over the years, getting readers involved with the quilting process had become very personal to her. She didn't want to screw it up by not managing her time well or failing to keep her promise. Her readers were just as invested in the success of the quilt as she was. She knew it, as evidenced by their heartfelt letters of love, loss, and redemption. She wouldn't let them down, even if it meant sleepless nights to get the quilt put together.

Molly had taken to quilting when she turned sixteen. One of the ladies in her church, Nora Johnson, took the awkward, self-conscious teenaged Molly under her wing. At first, the act of sewing gave Molly something to immerse herself in. Always quiet and withdrawn in school, she had few friends and few interests outside of reading and writing. Her parents tried to get her excited about other pursuits, but her childhood allergies kept her on the sidelines. She had trouble participating in sports, and on a personal level, didn't like anything with lots of loud noise or that made her stand out in public. She admired those who liked those types of activities, they simply weren't her cup of tea.

Nora had cajoled Molly into joining her group, eight women of all ages who loved to sew and create beautiful, lasting treasures. At first, she'd been quiet and tentative, absorbing every step in the quilting process. Hung in there a good three months before she let her guard down around the ladies. Another three months later, her confidence in quilting grew and she opened up, allowing herself to become a true part of the group. Quilting soon became her passion. Fourteen years later, she still met with the ladies as frequently as her work schedule allowed.

They'd been there for the important milestones in her life: wiping tears when Brad, her first love, had broken up with her the day before prom, celebrating when she graduated in the top 5 percent of her high school graduating class. They even took her on a special graduation trip in the summer to the National Quilt Museum in Kentucky.

During college, she met with them whenever she wasn't bogged down by studies and returned to the fold again when she went from intern to a Master's Publishing paid employee.

These women were the spiritual mothers and sisters of her heart, encouraging her in her job as well as her faith journey with the Lord. Oh, she'd had her ups and downs, questioning God's love for her at a young age until she accepted God's unconditional love and made Him the center of her life. She sought the Lord daily in all she did, knowing her walk with God kept her steady and grounded. She still wondered what her future path would be, but because of her relationship with God and her friends, she'd become a better person. A more confident woman, eager to follow God's plans for her life. She thanked God for her quilting friends and the joy they'd brought to her life.

Whenever she assembled a quilt, Molly experienced a sense of accomplishment, much like her brother must have felt when he brought home trophies and accolades for his participation on the high school football and track teams. Instead of trophies, Molly's joy came from knowing the quilts she and the ladies stitched went to help others, whether through gifts or auctioned off to help the community.

She fingered a swatch of soft pink fabric, remembering Ben asking if he would work on her special quilt. She snorted. Right. Like she'd let him touch her pet project. No, Nora and the ladies would find plenty to keep him busy once they had Ben in their clutches.

"This is far from over," she said to the quiet room, a surprising new energy zinging through her. All because of a crazy competition. She had to admit, she liked it.

—❦—

By the time Molly arrived at her parents' house, it was close to eight p.m. She'd proofread an article on historical quilts submitted by a contributing writer. The art director called, needing additional pictures for the next issue, and she'd put together notes for tomorrow's meeting with the staff in charge of the electronic version of *Quilter's Heart*.

She removed her jacket to enjoy the balmy evening and made her way to the house. Her father, James, had the door open before she stepped onto the landing.

"Hey, kiddo. Paul said you'd be stopping by."

She cringed at the nickname her father insisted on using. She preferred to be called Molly, but her father had taken to using the pet name years ago. Since it was the only thing in their awkward relationship to bind them together, she put up with it.

"I need to talk to him."

"He's out back."

Molly walked down the hallway, through the kitchen. Her mother must have made spaghetti sauce for dinner. Savory spices still scented the air. She stepped out to the screened enclosed patio to find her brother stretched out on a chaise lounge. One arm rested on the pillow centered on his chest, swaddled in a sling, the other held a copy of *Outdoor Adventures*.

She tamped down a surge of annoyance.

He glanced up from the magazine. "Hey. You made it."

"Sorry. Work took longer than usual tonight."

"You always work late?" he asked as he closed the magazine and focused his attention on her.

"Depends on what's going on." She pulled a metal chair from the outdoor dining set beside Paul. "What are you doing reading Ben's magazine?"

"Mom got it for me. Said it's from your publishing company." He held it up. "Pretty good, too."

Of course. She silently groaned.

"So, Sis, you've had me worried all afternoon. What's this important favor you need?"

"I need help learning how to kayak."

Paul blinked at her. "Come again?"

"Kayak. You know, canoe boat thingy you move with paddles."

"Yeah, I know what it is. Didn't think you did."

"Funny."

"You, in the great outdoors, kayaking? Now that's funny."

She pressed her lips together to keep from retorting with a scalding sibling remark. *Remember, you want the promotion.* "Except I'm serious."

Paul laid the magazine on the table beside the lounge and pushed himself upright, protecting his shoulder as he moved. "Kayaking, huh?"

"You can keep repeating it, but it won't change the facts."

"Why the sudden interest in water sports?"

"It's not my interest. It's my boss's idea." She gave her brother the particulars. "If I want the job, I have to excel and since you've always done so well at sports, and you're home, I thought you could give me some pointers. Maybe train me?"

"Wow. Never thought we'd be having this conversation." He stared at her. "Are you sure you want the job?"

"Yes." She sighed. "Look, the allergies are under control with shots and everything, so I shouldn't have a problem. Besides, I don't have much of a choice. Ben is just as motivated as I am. I need an edge here and you're it."

"Ben?" He glanced at the magazine he'd just set down. "Is he the competition?"

"Yeah. Ben Weaver. A real outdoors guy."

Paul frowned in thought. "Ben Weaver. I've heard the name before."

"You might have caught him on the television show *Extreme Survivors.*"

"Oh, yeah. Now I remember." He shook his head. "He's gonna be tough to beat."

"I know."

Paul went silent, staring out over the lanai. Trickling water, meant to be calming, bubbled down a rock pile before emptying into a small pool. Molly caught herself holding her breath, hoping her brother would say yes to her request. When he turned back, light shone in his eyes. "I'll help on one condition."

Here it comes. "What?"

"You make a baby quilt for a buddy of mine. His wife is due in about five months. Your quilts are nice and I'd like to give them a special gift."

She sat back in her chair, stunned. Paul thought her quilts were nice? He must have noticed her surprised reaction, because he went on to say, "Miss Nora from church sends me pictures of your projects with a care package from time to time. You're very talented."

"Thanks."

Nora had never mentioned corresponding with Paul, but it didn't surprise Molly. The older woman had her fingers in lots of activities at church. Writing to a serviceman would only be one of them.

"So? What do you say?" he asked. "Am I gonna be your coach in exchange for a baby quilt?"

"I say yes. I'd be honored to make a quilt for your friend and to have you as my coach."

He grinned. "You do realize we have our work cut out for us? I won't be easy on you."

The strange sense of excitement crept over her again. With Paul's input, she might do well after all. "I don't expect otherwise, but I promise to give it my all and not complain."

"Of course you'll give your all. You're a Henderson. It's what we do. But don't make any promises on the complaining part. It's gonna be tough training."

Molly smoothed her skirt, refusing to look at her brother. His words touched a nerve. She'd always felt lacking when it came to her family. "Sounds strange."

"What?"

"Being included as a tough Henderson."

Paul laughed. "You don't remember all the times you tried to keep up with me when you were little? How about when you first learned to ride a bike?"

"Not really."

"You were doing good, up until the time you wiped out. Scraped your elbows and knees."

She vaguely remembered the incident. Probably explained her aversion to playing outside.

"Anyway, we'll make a good team."

"Think so?"

"I'll make sure."

She nodded to his arm. "Will your injury be a problem?"

"I won't be able to get in the kayak with you, but I have a buddy who can help us out. It'll be up to you then."

"What is up to Molly?" their father asked as he and her mother, Cece, stepped into the screened porch to join them.

"Molly is going to learn to kayak."

Her father blinked, exchanged a puzzled glance with his wife.

Already sensing her parents' disapproval, Molly held up her hand. "Don't say it. Yes, it's true. I'm going to kayak."

Her dad glanced at Paul who nodded. "She's entering a competition and I'm gonna help her."

"Molly, last time you went on an outing during allergy season you were wheezing for weeks. You had trouble breathing and ended up at the ER," her mother reminded her in a stilted tone.

"Mom, it was years ago. I'll have my meds with me in case anything happens. Not only can I do this, but I'm going to be good at it."

"Why on earth, after all these years, would you take on an outdoor hobby?"

"It's more than a hobby." She waved off her mother's concern. No matter Molly's reasons for participating, her mother would exasperate her with a litany of explanations on why Molly shouldn't chance it.

"It's already settled. Paul and I are training. Well, I'm training. He's coaching. But the point is, we're doing something together."

As she'd hoped, her mother's mouth clamped shut when she learned of Paul's involvement. Molly may have silenced the woman for now, but had no doubt she'd hear about it later.

Her father sat with them, looking confused. "Why are you doing this?" he asked, picking up where her mother left off.

Molly had no choice but to explain the new dilemma in her life or never leave the house. She sighed as her mother asked, "Can Mr. Masterson do that?"

"He signs my paychecks."

Her father frowned. "It doesn't sound like a good idea."

She couldn't decide how to respond. Tell her dad what he wanted to hear? She'd be safe and not to worry? Like saying it would assure them. They'd been worrying about her for her entire life. The underlying threat of poor health always had her parents on edge. Even though she'd grown up, she still had to prove she could take care of herself.

"Dad, I'll be okay. I'm looking forward to the challenge." She'd made her stand, now she felt bolder. "I plan to show Ben Weaver, and the Henderson family, what I'm made of."

Her father blinked. "If you're sure."

"Oh, I'm sure I'm in over my head." She laughed. "But I have my big brother on my side, so yeah, I'm going through with it."

A slow grin spread over her father's face. "Well, good luck then,"

Molly stood, smiling as she felt the weight of the challenge grow a bit lighter. She stepped over to her father and kissed him on his cheek. "Thanks, Dad. I can't tell you how much your support means to me."

"So," Paul asked. "When do you want to start?"

"As soon as possible. Saturday? I know it's short notice, but I need to get started."

"I'll call my friend. He's got the equipment and will fill in wherever I can't because of my shoulder."

"Thanks, Paul."

"I'm gonna enjoy bossing you around, Sis." Paul swung his legs off the lounge chair and stood to join her, wrapping his good arm around her neck. "It'll be fun hanging out with my little sister."

"And I look forward to spending time with you, too."

As she said the words, Molly realized how much she meant them. How much she'd missed her brother. If nothing else, time together might launch a new beginning for them.

"I'll walk you out," her mother said as Molly collected her purse. At the front door, she stopped Molly from leaving by placing a firm hand on her arm. "I can't help but think you'll regret this decision. What if you get hurt? Or worse, miss work because you get sick? You aren't thinking, Molly."

Taking a deep breath, Molly squared her shoulders and clenched her fists. "On the contrary, Mom. I'm living. For the first time in a long time. All I ask is for you to believe in me."

"Then what about Paul?" her mother asked, trying a different tactic. "Aren't you concerned about his convalescence? What if he overuses his arm and delays the healing in his shoulder? He's on leave for a short while. I don't want to see him hurt in any way."

And there you had it. Her mother's concern for Paul. No motherly support for her.

"Don't worry, Mom. Next time I get myself into a bind, I'll wait until Paul leaves before I break my neck."

3

Ben would be arriving any minute. Although Molly relished the idea of watching Ben face her quilting group, she couldn't remember the last time she'd been so nervous. Trying to ignore the knots in her stomach, she tugged at the boxy dove gray jacket she'd paired with a pastel pink shell and dark denim jeans. Even though it was Thursday evening and she wasn't on the clock, in her mind, getting Ben squared away with her friends still constituted work, so she dressed accordingly.

"Like I told you," she repeated to Nora, "Ben is very confident. He's going to come in here sure he can master assembling a quilt on his very first try."

Nora Johnson, the longtime leader of the group, chuckled. Her soft, gray hair curved around her gentle face. Ocean-green eyes crinkled at the corners. Hopefully, her gentle face would lull Ben into complacency. But Molly knew under the kind exterior was a woman who had a keen eye for character. "You told us, dear. Five times."

"I just want to make sure you understand. He wants to win the challenge as much as I do."

"Calm down," said Janelle, a young mother who had joined the group a year ago. "We have your back."

"Just ignore the bull's-eye there and we'll be fine," Molly muttered.

The ladies began to chatter as they pulled out the multiple quilts in progress. For years now, they'd met at Nora's home. Her late husband had built an addition onto their house so Nora and her friends could indulge in their passion. The workroom contained two tables used for cutting fabric, both large enough to spread out a finished quilt top when ready to pin the batting and the back before stitching the pieces together. Of the two sewing machines, one had a long arm for large projects, the other used for embroidery. Shelves mounted on one entire wall held a vast assortment of supplies, from rulers and thread and needles, to graph paper and marking pencils. Natural light poured in through a large window. Between the mingled scents of brewed coffee wafting in from the kitchen and Nora's floral perfume, contentment filled Molly. Watching these women busy themselves cutting fabric or basting layers of a quilt together, Molly took comfort knowing she had her very own support team.

Even a team needed to go over the ground rules, however. It had been one day since Mr. Masterson issued his challenge, but she came prepared.

"As I discussed with Nora, starting Ben at the very beginning of the quilting process should keep him busy for a while. Even though we picked out a moderate pattern, I'm hoping he won't get the hang of it too soon."

"If he does, we'll move him on to something advanced," quipped Janelle.

Molly grinned then glanced at the worktable supporting the mound of folded fabric, cutting mat, pattern templates, and rotary cutter awaiting her nemesis.

"I plan on taking him through all the steps at a quick pace," Nora assured her, "from prep to final stitch. He'll be too busy to worry about what you're up to."

"Good. I should have my first kayak lesson Saturday. I hope I don't drown before this competition is over."

Miss Anne, another older woman in the group chuckled. "A competition involving a kayak and a quilting group. Your publisher has a wicked sense of humor."

"Don't I know it."

"And Molly asked her brother for help," Nora told the group. The women went silent, staring at her. Janelle dropped her scissors, its harsh metal clanking on the tile floor. Miss Anne's hand flew to her lips.

Nora cleared her throat to break the tension.

"So he's in town?" Janelle asked. "And he agreed to help?"

Molly downplayed it. "I need help. He's athletic."

"And you're family," Nora added. "God always has a way of bringing people together."

Ever since Molly could remember, Nora had been the cheerleader of the group, as well as the spiritual epicenter. Not much passed by the shrewd woman she didn't pray about accordingly. Molly had brought her problems to Nora and the women more times than she could count. The way things were going, she didn't expect to stop anytime soon.

"After all is said and done, we'll see how well my determination plays out." Molly strode to a workstation already laid out for Ben. "Remember, use as much quilting jargon as you can. Leave him on his own as much as possible. And please, don't let him charm you into sewing anything for him. I've seen him work a room. He's good at getting what he wants."

Miss Anne grinned. With rosy cheeks and short curly hair, she had the smile of an angel. And the temperament of a scamp. "Let's not be too hasty. It's been a long time since I had a man in my life."

"Anne," Nora warned. "Behave."

"I'm just saying." Miss Anne shrugged.

Having already debriefed the ladies, Molly knew they were prepared in any way to help her win the competition. Now, she had to pull herself together if she had any chance of beating Ben at their publisher's game.

Ben may be ahead of her in confidence, but she could be tenacious to a fault. After all, she talked Mr. Masterson into letting her start *Quilter's Heart*. She'd done her due diligence—from the number crunching to preparing a presentation and playing up her years as a faithful employee—and had gotten the man to take a chance on launching a new magazine in financially tough times. Since then she'd made it a successful magazine, a benefit to the publisher. Now, with her chance at a promotion, she wouldn't let nerves hold her back.

When Molly called Nora last night, they'd brainstormed for an hour, coming up with the perfect plan to let Ben see he wouldn't win without a fight. Molly didn't consider herself to have a mean bone in her body, but she had to admit, she couldn't wait for the torture to begin.

"Are you sure the pattern we picked will keep Ben guessing?"

"After you mentioned he thought the quilt in your office resembled a jigsaw puzzle, I found a twisted spool pattern to stump him."

She began to pace. "Good. Good."

"Molly, calm down." Nora patted her arm. "We have everything under control. You have to have faith."

Molly blew out a breath. "I do."

"My dear, Ben will be so over his head, he'll think he can't finish the project. And of course, no decent project can be done fast. You know we don't tolerate sloppy work, so he won't slide by."

Molly straightened her shoulders. "Okay. Piece of cake. We can do this."

Nora chuckled. "Of course *you* can."

"Thanks."

"I believe in you. All you have to do is believe in yourself. The Lord will guide you, just wait and see."

"I have been keeping Him busy with my prayers."

"He hears, so stop worrying."

If only she could. Molly believed the Lord would take care of her, but she had her own part to play. She kept telling herself the more she yanked herself out of her comfort zone, the better the results would be. Time would tell if her new attitude would be enough to get the promotion or humiliate her to the *nth* degree.

"So tell me, how is the Hearts Entwined quilt coming along?"

Back to a topic she loved. Molly relaxed. "The amount of fabric I received turned out better than I had anticipated. And the stories? Sure to touch the readers' hearts. As I read them all, one thing stood out. Women, from different places and stages of life, experience the same issues, pain, and triumphs. It connects us all. Ties our lives together.

"I was able to cut all the pieces for the heart patterns and still have some left over. I'm thinking about incorporating the remnants into the border somehow. Or maybe the corner squares if I have time."

"Think you'll have it done in time for the Expo?"

"If I have to work long nights to finish, then yes."

"You should have brought it tonight. We could have helped you with it."

"Thanks, but I'm doing some of the stitching at work to keep the staff up-to-date and then working at home. You know how territorial I get about my projects."

Nora shook her head. "You are stubborn."

Molly grinned. "So I've been told."

"At least the trait will work in your favor."

Unlike in times past. Molly had never had an easy relationship with her parents. She tended to take a stand on topics she knew they wouldn't see eye-to-eye on. Instead of telling her how proud they were of her career success, they compared everything to what her brother did. When she'd started volunteering for Second Chances, her parents were concerned for her safety, worried an abusive husband might storm the center looking for his wife or the long hours she put in might leave her vulnerable to strangers taking advantage of her kindness. Not trying to allay their fears, she jumped right in, helping abused women any way she could. She might not be fighting for her country the way Paul did, but she had her own way of helping. Once she started, her heart went out to these women and there was no way she'd back off just because her folks wanted her to.

Organizations like Second Chances benefited from the Expo. The money from the auctioned items went into a general fund and was dispersed evenly, or any bidder could pick one organization to donate to. Molly hoped the proceeds from the Hearts Entwined quilt went to her pet cause. Even if she had to put up some of her own money.

From inside the house, the doorbell rang. Ben. Molly's stomach twisted. Yes, nerves were at the forefront, but curiosity had her looking forward to spending time with him outside of the office.

"Molly, dear. Why don't you get the door?" Nora suggested.

Molly swallowed hard. Game time.

Ben took one look at the guarded faces before him and knew he'd just entered enemy territory. The usual excitement pumping him up before an event deserted him. Normally, he faced male opponents, although he'd been up against some tough female competitors a time or two. He'd been in his element then, ready to push his body to the max during a sporting event or outdoor challenge. He always played to win. At all costs. And while he'd found himself in some pretty tricky circumstances over the years, nothing prepared him for the homey, feminine atmosphere.

Suck it up, Weaver. It'll be worth it in the end.

His gaze swept around the room as he gauged his surroundings. Nothing in the room looked familiar. What had he expected? The type of outdoor equipment he worked with on a regular basis? Instead, he came face-to-face with sewing machines and fabric, thread lined up in a spool holder mounted on the wall. Maybe he should have done a little research before coming here tonight instead of going home first to change into more comfortable jeans and T-shirt.

Suddenly, he wasn't so sure about his part in the challenge.

He ramped up his smile to hide his concern from the grandmother and sisterly types, smiling at him with sweet angelic faces. How scary could they be? Besides, he'd be working with them for a short while. Once he got the promotion, he'd be spending a lot more time in the office. He'd have the day-to-day running of the magazine to worry about, not like now, wondering if he could sit here for hours, sewing. Budget reports, production issues, and working with a much larger staff looked a whole lot better than what these women had in store for him.

He shook off his doubts. How hard could it be to work with a bunch of women? He liked women as much as the next guy, but to think they'd help him get the promotion? Probably a stretch. A mile-long stretch.

"Ben, I'd like you to meet the ladies." Molly introduced each one and each one smiled back at him, wary expressions on their faces. Nora looked friendly enough. Surely, she would take pity on him. And the other two women? Their expressions varied from mischief to disapproval. Given enough time, could he finesse them? *Treat them like old buddies and win them over, Weaver.* He'd done it before to get a story—he could do it again. Only now, he had more than a story at stake.

He met Molly's gaze. When he glimpsed the twinkle in her eye, he swallowed hard, knowing for all his rational thinking, he was in deep trouble.

"So, Ben, tell us about yourself," said Nora, winning him over with her kind eyes.

"I . . . um . . . ," he stuttered, at a loss for words.

"What Ben is so succinctly trying to say is, he's editor of *Outdoor Adventures*. He participates in extreme sports or other kinds of adventures, like underwater cave exploration or driving race cars, all in the name of getting a story."

Nora frowned. "Oh dear. I'm afraid we don't have anything exotic to offer you."

"I realize that," Ben rushed to reassure her. "I admit, I've never taken part in a quilting bee, but it's never too late to learn a new skill."

He swore Molly snorted at his remark, but when he glanced her way, she portrayed innocence.

"You'll do just fine," Nora gave him a tender pat to the arm. He went still, wondering at the strange sensation. It had been so long since someone touched him with motherly concern. "We're going to take you through the steps of quilt making. Rotary cutting, assembling, and hand-stitching the blocked quilt top, basting top and back together and embroidery. Before long, you'll be using the long arm."

He frowned. "The what?"

Nora pointed to the machine. "It's got all the bells and whistles."

"And the NTS is automatic," Janelle piped in.

"Sounds dangerous."

Molly chuckled. "Rich, coming from the adventure guy."

"By the time we finish the quilt," Nora went on to say, "you'll be almost as good as our Molly."

"Nobody's as good as Molly with a needle and thread," Miss Anne told him. "She's won two state fair ribbons for her work. She'd have more projects going, if she had more time to herself."

"She's been designing her own patterns for quite a while now," Janelle said. "My goodness, her creations are so detailed, they look like photographs instead of material. You can't believe the talent behind her precise needlework."

Ben noticed the slight blush on Molly's cheeks. Not one to accept compliments?

"Come on," she protested. "You all have won awards too."

"But none as prestigious as yours," Anne countered. "Why, the last pattern you designed was a work of art. Not just anyone could have come up with it."

Molly smiled, pride shining in her eyes.

"I won an award," Ben blurted, then wished he'd kept his mouth shut when four pairs of eyes zeroed in on him. He could have sworn his face heated up.

"How wonderful. For what?" Nora asked.

"Baseball. When I was a kid." His father had coached his Little League teams during his childhood and had been Ben's biggest fan during high school. To him, the trophy he and his dad received had been the most precious thing in his life, right after the ball his dad caught at an Orioles game just before he died.

"Nothing more serious?" Janelle asked. "Like an Emmy or Pulitzer?"

Molly closed her eyes and shook her head.

His collar grew warm. Lame. What made him share the little piece of his history? Like these ladies cared. Not with Miss Perfect Quilt Molly in their midst.

Anne blinked. "Well, we all appreciate a little recognition in our life. No matter how long ago."

He shifted in place, not sure how to proceed after making a fool of himself.

"Wonderful, dear." Nora tapped her hand on the worktable. "But now it's time to get started. If you come over here, Ben, you'll see we have your all your supplies set out."

He approached the table. Okay, he could relate to getting everything in order before starting a new quest. Same with quilting, he realized. He recognized the folded fabric and a ruler, but not the cardboard cutouts. And why did you need a pizza cutter? He picked it up, turned to Molly, brow raised.

"Rotary cutter. Makes it easy to cut fabric when you have the templates laid out." She lifted the cutouts, explaining them to him like he was a first grader, then reached for a picture of the completed quilt project. "See how all these strips of fabric make up a block? You follow the color pattern, make enough of these blocks, and you have a quilt top."

"Like the one I saw in your office?"

"Sort of. My pattern is a lot more detailed. With yours, you'll mix colors to make the pattern."

"So you're saying I have to walk, before I can run."

"Right. In your vernacular, you have to work up to the big play. You wouldn't run a 5k without practice, right? Same principle, different implementation. So start cutting."

"The fabric?"

She handed him the cardboard templates. "Just follow the pattern."

"We're starting you off with the basics," Nora told him. "Quilting 101."

Molly put the picture aside and shook out the fabric on the table, smoothing the wrinkles as she went, as if the fabric was a priceless commodity instead of what he assumed was cotton.

He tightened his grip around the cutter. "Right now?"

"Better late than never."

Before he had a chance, Janelle sidled up to him. "My husband saw you on TV." She leaned against the worktable, arms crossed over her chest, eyes narrowed. "I think it was the show where you went marlin fishing. He talked about going deep sea fishing for a month afterwards."

"He should try it." Finally, something Ben had knowledge about. Enthused, he continued. "It's pretty exciting. Your body gets a real workout. Struggling with the catch is a rush."

"My husband is an accountant." She informed him, her foot tapping at a rapid pace. "Trust me, he's much safer on land than anywhere near water. He'd land face first in the Gulf of Mexico and I'd never hear the end of it, like it was my fault instead of his crazy idea."

So much for finding safe conversation. Judging by Janelle's tone, her husband wasn't much of an outdoorsman.

"Oh dear."

From the other side of the worktable, Molly looked up from the pattern pieces she was studying. "What's wrong, Nora?"

Distracted, the older woman rummaged through Ben's pile of fabric, then hurried to a rolling bin and pulled out a drawer. "I feel as though I've forgotten something, but for the life of me can't think of it."

Ben noticed the concern on Molly's face. Was it his imagination or did she look prettier out of the office?

"Never mind. I'll think of it later." Nora waved a hand, as if forgetting was not a big deal. "Molly, step away from the table and let Ben work. You're hovering. It's his task, remember?"

When Molly blushed again, Ben hid a smile.

"He's way behind the curve here," Nora said. "And to be quite honest, I don't want to be here all night holding his hand."

Yep. So much for making the process painless.

The ladies spent the next hour working on various projects, interrupting Ben from time to time to draw him away from cutting fabric in order to demonstrate a quilting technique. While he tried to pay attention, he kept Molly in his peripheral vision, catching her gaze from time to time as she glanced at him. Tonight she'd dressed in jeans, a different look from the office. He liked it. Distracted enough by her presence, he went on overload trying to concentrate on all the different aspects of quilting. At this rate, he'd never get anything done.

When Janelle announced she had to head home and relieve her husband from babysitting duties, he breathed a sigh of relief. So far lesson one hadn't been too bad. At least he still had all his fingers.

He gathered up the cut fabric to place in a pile when Molly came up beside him.

"Before we call it a night, I have something for you." He turned to find her holding out a thick book, offering it to him like a peace offering. "Homework. *Quilting A-Z*. Study and learn."

She plopped it in Ben's reluctant hands with way too much relish.

"Bet you wish you had a big lead right about now."

4

The next morning, Molly stepped off the elevator into the lobby of Master's Publishing, juggling her purse, briefcase, and a to-go cup of coffee, and came to a screeching halt. Against the half-wall once housing a reception desk, someone had placed a table. A large trophy sat in the center with a laminated sign placed beside it. On closer inspection, she read her name and Ben's in bold letters along with the caption, Who Will Win Masterson's Machination?

"Oh, please," she groaned. Shaking her head, she beelined to her office, intercepted by Taylor on the way.

"Like it?"

"The trophy or the name? They're both a bit much, don't you think?"

"No, it's great. Charlie found the trophy in a storage closet and dragged it out for inspiration."

"I remember. The city baseball league the office participated in a few years ago."

"Yep. We're not above recycling."

As they crossed the main floor, other coworkers, all women, called out good luck to Molly.

"We all have your back," Taylor said.

51

"And if I lose?"

"Get the thought right out of your mind. You will win and the women will be triumphant. And win the grand prize."

In her office, Molly dropped her bags on a chair and set her coffee on her desk. "There's a grand prize?"

"Charlie and I had a meeting, you know, as representatives from both sides of the table. I came up with the name; don't let Charlie make you think otherwise. He's not very clever. Anyway, we asked everyone to chip in some extra bucks. Either the guys or girls will use the money to go out for a nice lunch after the winner is announced." She grinned. "Bragging rights are free."

"You have this all figured out, don't you."

Taylor planted her hands on her hips. "You bet."

Molly removed her lemon yellow suit jacket and slipped it over the back of her chair before sitting. "I'm surprised to see Charlie involved."

"Me too. We were trash talking at the coffee station and one thing led to another. He's convinced Ben will win, hands down."

"So am I."

"Way to be a downer."

"Sorry, Taylor It's the stress talking." After a sleepless night, Molly's worries had rooted deeper. When sleep eluded her, she worked on the Hearts Entwined quilt for a few hours. By two a.m. she went to bed, tossing and turning until dawn.

Taylor plopped down in a chair opposite Molly's desk. "What's wrong?"

So many things. Where did she start? "I want the promotion. I've worked here a very long time and getting the position would be validation for the years I've put into the company. I'm not about to let a guy who showed up six months ago take the job I should have. It's a big step, but I know I'd make a good editor-in-chief if given the chance."

"But?"

Of course Taylor heard the unspoken but at the end of Molly's speech.

"But Ben is a worthy opponent. He's had more experience in the art of competition. Even though I don't work directly with him, he must know what he's doing or he'd never have gotten the editorial job, despite Mr. Masterson's obvious admiration for the guy. Granted, sewing may not be his strong suit, but he adapts. I don't."

"Since when?"

"Since always."

Taylor tilted her head. "Have you forgotten how hard you lobbied to start *Quilter's Heart*? You spent months working on the concept. When the focus group showed a positive response, you got the magazine up and running. No easy feat."

"It's my job."

"Doesn't mean it didn't take a lot of competitiveness on your part to pull it through. You focused, put your time and energy into the project, and made it successful. Think Mr. Masterson would consider you for editor-in-chief if you hadn't impressed him somewhere along the line?"

Molly had never looked at it that way. She'd always been a hard worker, ever since she tried to get her parents to notice her over her brother's accomplishments. She never put two and two together, wanting to be accepted by those around her made her competitive out of necessity.

Yes, she knew the business, otherwise Mr. Masterson wouldn't have given her a chance. He must have faith in her abilities. *So have faith in yourself.*

Even though she knew the main point of the challenge was for show, her boss hadn't gotten where he had in the business world without placing successful people in positions to benefit his publishing empire. He knew both Ben and Molly could handle the day-to-day operations of a magazine. Yet armed with enough knowledge, she still worried.

"Molly, you can't get ahead in our world unless you're competent. And have some gumption. You, my friend, have both in spades."

"Hmm." She smiled at her friend. "I appreciate your faith in me, but I haven't had my first kayaking lesson yet."

"Did you call your brother?"

"I did. He agreed to help. He's excited about coaching me."

"Awesome. Don't look at yourself as *not* being winning material, think of yourself as *the* winner. You will be." Taylor jumped up. "Need to get back to work. Remember, Fab Friday meeting at ten for all magazine editors."

Once Taylor left, Molly gathered the notes she'd compiled to review before the meeting. There were four other magazine editors based in the Tampa office. They held monthly meetings to go over publishing schedules and general magazine matters.

Unable to keep her mind on the task at hand, Molly stood, stretched, and ended up pulling her quilting project from the tote bag. She ran her fingers over the soft squares of material she'd already pieced together. Not far enough along as she'd like, but her excitement about the special quilt hadn't dimmed since she came up with the initial concept. She'd read every letter delivered to the office with the sample of fabric. Lost herself in each woman's story. Though varied, they all came down to one important component, the ability of women to triumph and carry on in times of hardship, loss, or pain. Molly hoped her vision would touch a few lives along the way.

She spread the quilt top over the table, grinning at the flannel material printed with ducks. The mother who sent in the fabric told the story of her premature labor. The reports had been negative, but the baby rallied and lived. He was now two years old and thriving. Other pieces included: bright pink satin, sent in by a mother who lost her daughter in a car accident on the way to prom; lace from a wedding gown sent in by a bride who almost lost her fiancé in Afghanistan; and a scrap of a tattered robe sent in by a daughter who sat at her mother's bedside, waiting for the beloved older woman to go home to the Lord.

So many stories from so many segments of life. She'd struggled over the way to match the pattern with each scrap of fabric. Similar stories together? Old and young separated? In the end, she decided every story touched her heart, so she didn't need a specific order. The darker colors would make up the shapes creating the top heart, the lighter colors would be the inverted heart.

The human heart withstood so much of life's victories and disappointments. The shared experiences of life would be the focal point, the heart and soul of the quilt. Could she find the courage and inner fortitude like these women to complete Mr. Masterson's challenge and come out the victor?

Determination swelled in her spirit.

One step at a time, she remembered Nora saying. Put one foot in front of the other and let God lead you through this journey called life. He would always be there for her, and so far, He hadn't let Molly down.

She itched to pick up her needle and thread right then and there to continue the project, but the pesky details of her job kept her from doing so. She smiled and took one last look at her work, gaining strength from the stories the quilt inspired. Maybe she could win.

The meeting ran longer than usual, right up to the lunch hour. Ben grabbed a sandwich from the restaurant on the street level, ten floors below his office. Taking his purchase to eat at one of the outside bistro tables and enjoy the fresh air on yet another warm spring day, he noticed Molly sitting at the farthest table talking on her phone.

He took a step to join her and hesitated. Should he dine with the enemy? He almost chuckled out loud at the thought. Molly? Right. She rated about as far from anyone's enemy as they came, but had become his rival when you came right down to it. One he'd have to keep an eye on. And since she was pleasing to his eyes, watching out for her didn't constitute much of a hardship.

Before he had a chance to decide, she stood and hurried to the entrance of the building, nearly colliding with him.

"Hey, where's the fire?"

She stopped. Blinked. "How did you know?"

His brows rose. "Know what?"

"About the fire?"

He took a step back and gazed up. "There's a fire? Upstairs?"

"No. At a woman's center I work with. It happened two weeks ago. We've run into all kinds of problems with the renovations. It's turning into a nightmare." She rubbed her temple. "I just got off the phone with the contractor. I volunteered to be the contact person for the project and he needs me at the location to review a new development."

"Now?"

She nodded. "The current director of the facility hasn't been . . . engaged with the problem."

Nice way to put it.

"I'm going over now." She glanced at her watch. "I should be able to get there and back before lunch hour ends."

"You look pretty stressed. How about I drive with you?"

She glanced at the bag in his hand. "Have you eaten yet?"

"No, but I could use a change of scenery besides the four walls of my office, so how about I tag along? Maybe I can help you with the contractor."

"Are you saying I can't handle a simple thing like answering a contractor's questions?" Her cheeks turned an appealing shade of pink.

Ben smiled. A fire lit in Molly whenever he questioned her abilities. He doubted she noticed her passionate reaction. Or how much he enjoyed annoying her.

"No, I just want to help."

She stared at him for a long moment and blew out a breath. "Hey, if you can help, I'm not too proud to let you talk to the contractor. All I care about is getting the center open again."

"Great. I'll drive."

"What about your food?"

"I'll get to it later." He took hold of her elbow, leading her to the parking garage and helped her into his SUV. Once she gave him the address, he punched it into the GPS and they were on the road. She called to tell her assistant she'd be late coming back from lunch.

"So what happened to the center?" he asked when she ended the call.

"Kitchen fire. Caused a lot of smoke damage and ruined everything. I never realized how long it can take for a cleanup project."

"Permits. Subcontractors. Time and money. It all adds up."

She glanced over at him.

"I have a buddy who builds houses." One of the few lasting friends from his childhood, before he cut everyone off after his parents' deaths. "He's vented about a job or two."

"Then it's a good thing you came along. I may be a quick study, but I'm not up on building codes."

A few minutes passed in silence as Ben drove through Tampa traffic.

"So," Ben ventured. "What's the name of the center?"

"Second Chances."

"How did you get involved?"

"It's a weird story."

"We have a few minutes."

"Okay." Molly angled in her seat toward him. "I was working late one night, about seven or so, when I headed to my car. As I went

57

to unlock the door, I heard what sounded like crying. I stopped to listen, but nothing. I started to open the car door when I heard it again. A woman's crying. Curious, I followed the sound and found a young woman huddled in the stairwell near the elevator bank."

"Pretty gutsy on your part to check it out by yourself. Could have been dangerous."

She shrugged. "I didn't think about it at the time. I just sensed someone needed help."

"So what happened?"

"Turns out the girl was a runaway. Believe me, it took a while to get her to open up, but I spoke to her in a soothing tone for a while so she wouldn't be afraid. She didn't want to tell me at first, but as we talked, I learned she'd had an argument with her boyfriend. By the faded bruises on her face, I'd say they'd had arguments before." Molly went silent. Ben looked over, catching the indignation on her face.

"Weren't you worried the guy might come looking for his girlfriend?"

"I was too incensed on her behalf to worry about danger. She was so scared he'd find her, she didn't know what to do."

"But you did?"

"I remembered hearing about Second Chances, from church, I think, so I asked if she wanted me to take her there. She hesitated. After some discussion, she decided to get help. We walked back to my car and then things got weird."

"Weirder than they already were?"

"You'd think, but no."

He couldn't wait to hear the rest.

"As we walked to my car, we heard a guy yelling from another level in the garage. His voice echoed and I have to say, he creeped me out. Her name was Jenny, and she freaked because the voice sounded like her boyfriend. She started to run. I went after her, followed her down the stairway and caught up to her. Got her to stop long enough to catch her breath and listen to me. I assured her we'd get back to my car in one piece, but we heard the guy's voice again, right above us, on the floor of the garage where I'd parked my car."

"Did she listen to you?"

Molly shook her head. "She wanted to take off, but I knew her boyfriend would find her if she went back out on the street. Grabbing her hand, we hurried to the elevator. I stabbed at the button and the door slid open, but the bell didn't ring. You know, the one that sounds when the door opens?"

He turned to look at her. "No way."

"Yes, way."

He couldn't deny the earnest expression on her face as she told the story with growing excitement. He'd never seen the animated side of Molly before and decided he liked it.

"So we went back up to my car. I made her get on the floor in the back then locked the doors. As I made it to the exit, I saw a guy pacing the sidewalk. Probably her boyfriend. Anyway, we got to the shelter safe and sound."

"I thought you said it was a center."

"There are two locations. The shelter is for women who need immediate help from an abusive partner. The center works with women ready to get back on their feet by offering training and support. We also have clothing donations so they have professional outfits to wear on job interviews."

"Gotcha."

"Here's the weird part."

"There's more to the story?"

She chuckled. "I ran into a repairman the next morning when I came into the office, fixing the elevator bell. It had been broken and I never even noticed it when I came to work the day before."

"Definitely weird."

"I went back to check on Jenny a day later. She'd decided to go home at the suggestion of the counselor who spent time with her.

She couldn't say enough about how being at the shelter saved her life. Seeing her safe and sound, ready to fix her life, well, I started volunteering."

"Do you help out at both places?"

"Mostly the center. I worked with the previous director so I know the ins and outs, but if needed, I can put time in at the shelter, too."

He gave Molly a sideways glance. This Molly, all buttoned-up and serious at work, had saved a young girl from her violent boyfriend? Seems he had a lot more to learn about Miss Molly.

Before long, they arrived at the center. Molly and the contractor, Tom, went straight to work. Despite her claim of not knowing what to do, she handled herself like a professional.

"Ben," she called to him. "Tom needs to find a new drywall subcontractor. Think your friend could help?"

"Let me call my buddy."

"Thanks." She beamed at him, and his chest grew tight. By her smile, she acted like he was a war hero who'd just saved the day. He'd just offered to call a friend who might help them. Nothing special to her.

But to him?

He pondered his reaction to her reaction. Downright strange for a guy who shied away from relationships, right? Especially romantic entanglements. He wasn't looking for a woman in his life at the moment, but Molly had caught his attention big-time.

Once Molly and the contractor finished their business, Ben escorted Molly back to the SUV, contemplating his moment of revelation. His musings were interrupted when his cell phone rang.

"Ben Weaver."

"Ben, this is Nora Johnson. You know, Molly's friend."

"Yes, Nora, I remember."

Molly swung around to face him, her brow wrinkled with concern.

"I'm afraid I have a bit of a problem for our quilting time tonight."

Right. Quilting. Ben had almost forgotten his standing date. Friday night spent with the quilting ladies. Man, he had to get a social life. "What's up?"

"I remembered I wanted to add another color to the fabric I picked out for your project. Would it be too much trouble for you to stop at Quilting Paradise for a yard of yellow material before you come over tonight? Nan at the counter can help you pick out what I need. I've spoken to her already."

"Sure."

"Look at the shopping trip as part of your learning curve."

He glanced at Molly, who stood beside him, arms crossed over her chest and a frown on her face.

Learning curve indeed.

5

Molly watched Ben slip his phone back into his slacks pocket. "Is Nora okay?"

"She's fine, but it seems I need your help now."

Surprise softened her features.

He explained Nora's request. "So my question is, will you come with me to the store? I don't even like to shop for clothes. Material? No clue."

"I'm not sure it's how the competition thing works. The idea is to work against each other." She sent him a sheepish smile. "But you did come with me to the center, so I guess it's okay one time."

"Even though it is challenge-related?"

"I don't think accompanying you to the store will make much of an impact."

"Couldn't hurt."

True. And if she spent more time with Ben, she could figure out his weaknesses and play them to her advantage. *Right. Like Ben has any weaknesses.*

The more she hung out with him, the more intrigued she became. A little too intrigued for her peace of mind. Still, the plan sounded good anyway.

She glanced at her watch, hoping to make it seem like she had trouble fitting him into her busy schedule. She couldn't make it too easy for him. "We can't swing it now. How about after work?"

Relief showed on his face. "Great. Meet at the elevators at five?"

Excitement she couldn't ignore tingled in her. "I'll be there."

Back at the office building, they went straight up to the tenth floor. As they stepped off the elevator, Molly touched Ben's arm. He looked at her hand, then her face.

"Thanks. For coming with me," she said, mesmerized by the heightened awareness between them.

His eyes went dark. "Anytime."

They stood for a moment, caught up in whatever the moment represented, until Charlie's voice broke it up.

"Hey you two. Glad you're together."

Like they'd been caught doing something wrong, fraternizing with the enemy, for instance, Ben took a step back. Molly tried not to let the move bother her, but it did just the same. While they'd had a nice time together, reality slapped her in the face. There was a real competition between them and if she wanted to move up in the company, she had to remember the facts. Getting lost in Ben's chocolate brown eyes and feeling all shivery around him wouldn't go very far in getting the promotion. They were adversaries, nothing more.

Striving for her best business voice, she said, "What's up, Charlie?"

"I got the details on a kayak excursion. It's a benefit for an organization helping troubled teens." He looked at Molly and grinned. "Your teammates are fresh out of juvenile detention."

~

Ben watched Molly's face pale before she excused herself and hurried to her office. He couldn't help feeling sorry for her. Another added pressure to her already overflowing plate. He turned to Charlie.

"How'd you manage finding this team?"

He shrugged. "Fell right into our hands. When I checked out the different kayaking trips best fitting our situation, I found a team-building group that plans events to help troubled youth. They'll meet to get to know each other before tackling the three-mile trip at the end of the month. How can Molly turn down the opportunity to vie for the challenge and help a good cause? Mr. Masterson will be all over it."

True. Masterson loved positive publicity and Charlie, eager to please, had honed in on the fact and played it to their advantage. He couldn't complain, yet he felt Molly had a definite disadvantage since she hadn't had her first lesson yet.

"Think it's a good thing putting pressure on Molly?"

"You want to win, don't you?"

Okay, here you had it. In order to proceed with his plans, which included setting down roots, making new friends and reconnecting with old ones, he needed the new job. He'd sworn nothing would get in his way, including Molly.

"She'll be so busy trying to stay upright in the boat and deal with the kids on her team, she'll run out of time. By then, you'll have this thing sewn up." Charlie chuckled at his own joke. "Sewn up. Because you're quilting. Get it?"

Ben grimaced. "Yeah, I get it."

"Anyway, I have the details all laid out in your office."

"Thanks."

"And I took the liberty of picking out a few nice restaurants for you to pick from. You know, when the guys win the office wager."

The office wager. He'd forgotten, but the staff had not.

A banner hung over the Molly's office door, bold red letters proclaiming, "You go Girl!" Every desk occupied by a female held a small, red flag with a pink heart in the center, attached to a short stick placed in pencil holders. These women were all in for their girl.

"Don't mind all this stuff," Charlie told him as they passed by the decorated desks on the way to his office. "We've got something better."

Ben wasn't sure he wanted to know what constituted better, but found out when he reached his office. A speaker, mounted on the wall above the door announced, "Ben's the man" in a prerecorded voice when he opened the door. A chorus of males around the office responded with, "Oh yeah, Ben's the man."

He shot Charlie an incredulous glance. "You're kidding me, right?"

"Our battle cry. Brilliant, if I do say so myself." Charlie held up a placating hand. "We have to be a constant reminder, man. Get in their heads. Mess with them."

"You are one troubled dude."

"But I get the job done."

Ben entered his office and closed the door behind him, grateful he didn't hear his name over the speaker again. He dreaded opening the door again to leave. How long did the guys think he would tolerate his name blaring across the office? Not long at all, if he had any say in the matter.

Shaking his head, he took a seat behind his desk and went through the paperwork Charlie had left him. Articles, advertising, and budget reports took his mind off the challenge at hand for a good hour. When he came across the information on the kayak trip, he took his time reading.

Troubled kids and their families participated in activities to encourage the kids to make better choices. They encouraged mentors to get involved and spend time with the kids. It sounded good, a community project their boss would embrace. But would Molly be up to it? And why was he worried about her? She'd more than assured him she could handle the challenge. Shouldn't he be worried about his own part?

Molly's pretty face flashed across his mind as he tossed the paper on his desk. In light of her part in the challenge, he was glad Molly had time to practice. At first, he thought he was being magnanimous suggesting he give her a head start, knowing she didn't have the physical stamina for any real athletic endeavor. The thought of her pale skin turning red in the sun, or her sustaining an injury gnawed at him. His inner guy code might want to protect her, but after having spent time with her, he recognized the determined gleam in her eyes. She just might make it on brute stubbornness alone.

Still, he couldn't ignore the niggling concern. Surely, she wouldn't get in over her head just to prove she deserved the new position? Why couldn't she have been given a different task? One more within her reach, like badminton? Oh, right, because *he* happened to be doing an issue on kayaking. If anything happened to her, he'd deserve the blame.

Just before five, he tidied his desk, turned off the lights, and left his office, being serenaded once again by the speaker calling out his name. A few men replied with, "Ben's the man." As much as he enjoyed the camaraderie, the speaker had to go.

He met Molly at the elevator, a sassy smile on her lips.

"Go ahead," he told her. "Say it."

"I'll take the quiet banner over a loudspeaker any day."

"You and me both. I plan on disconnecting it tomorrow."

She chuckled and stepped in the elevator when it arrived. "Do you know where the store is?"

He pressed the button for the garage level. "Yes. I set the GPS."

"You GPS everything?"

He leaned against the wall. "Since returning to Tampa, I've had to get acclimated again to the area. Coming in and out of town, I didn't have to worry too much about getting many places. Now I do."

"Is it strange staying in town for good?"

"I like it."

"Haven't gone stir crazy?"

"Only when I'm cutting fabric."

She chuckled. "Good point."

The elevator doors slid open. "See you there," Molly called over her shoulder as she headed to her sedan.

The late afternoon traffic kept Ben tangled up until he arrived at Quilter's Paradise, just behind Molly. When they stepped in the door, Molly stopped short and took a deep breath.

"Something wrong?"

"It's the store. I love the scent of fabric." Her cheeks turned a charming shade of pink, as if she'd just revealed a deep, dark secret about herself.

Ben gazed around the cozy store with a frown.

"Something wrong?" Molly parroted.

"I've never been in a fabric store. Where do we start?"

"Don't worry, I know my way around here blindfolded."

"I'll bet you do," he muttered.

"Hey, I'd feel the same way in a Bass Pro Shop."

He glanced at her with a grin. "You know the name. I'm impressed."

She shrugged. "It's called research."

Their gazes tangled. A strong sensation stirred in his gut.

Molly blinked. "So . . . um . . . let's find Nan."

"Back here," Nan called out from her station behind the register. "I've been expecting you." As they drew closer, Nan chuckled. "Well, him anyway, not you Molly."

Molly made introductions. "Ben persuaded me he needed my help."

Nan winked. "Right."

"So, Nora called?" Molly asked, refusing to look at him. She grabbed hold of a sewing doodad on the counter and fidgeted with it while she spoke to the store owner. He wasn't sure why, but he liked the fact he had an effect on her.

"She wanted me to assist Ben in selecting the fabric," Nan said, "but since you came out of your way, I'm sure you can do it." The store phone rang. "Just let me know when you need it cut."

"Thanks, Nan."

Like an expert, Molly wove her way through the store to the fabric section. Myriad bolts set up in coordinating colors lined the shelves.

"Look at all this material," he said.

"It's a quilting shop. Can't make quilts without fabric."

"I have no idea where to start."

"Broadcloth should do."

They stopped beside the yellow-hued section. Ben stuffed his hands in his pockets, his brow creased.

"Problem?" she asked, sweet as sugar.

"Slight."

"Just pick out something to go with the fabric you cut out yesterday."

"There's the problem. I don't remember what it looks like."

Her brows angled in a perplexed look. "How could you not remember? You spent hours cutting."

"I was so concerned about cutting the fabric just like the template, I didn't notice the colors."

She chuckled. "This challenge gets better and better."

Ben stepped closer and pointed to a shade he thought matched the fabric back at Nora's. Molly shook her head then tilted it to the right. Ben turned back to the choices before him and pointed to the next bolt. She took two steps to the right. He pointed to another bolt, two away from the last.

She smiled at his choice.

"You couldn't just tell me which one to pick?"

"In the spirit of the competition, no."

He lifted the bolt from its resting place. "I get it."

"Remember my kindness when the kayaking starts."

While Ben brought the fabric to the cutting table, Molly wandered. He watched her stroll through the red and pink section, then come to a sudden stop. After a few moments of what appeared to be heavy deliberation, she tugged a bolt loose from the shelf and carried it to the cutting table. A bright red with tiny pink hearts.

Ben shot her a curious look.

"For my special project. The colors are perfect for the backing."

"Ah. Shouldn't you be more worried about kayaking?"

"I should be, but I can't pass it up."

"Okay then."

They made their purchases and strolled to the parking lot. Homebound traffic buzzed by in the main street. A slight breeze lifted a strand of Molly's hair. When she raised her hand to smooth it down, Ben noticed her elegant fingers. Fingers used to create a work of art. He liked her ability to bring beauty into the world without realizing just how her gift touched others. Him included. Why had he never noticed before?

"So, you're off to Nora's?" she asked as they stopped beside their vehicles.

"She's expecting me."

Molly sent him a mischievous grin.

The look sent a shot of concern down his spine. "Should I be concerned?"

"No. I believe it's just the two of you tonight."

"And this is a bad thing?"

"It is if you don't want to talk about yourself, which I've noticed you don't like to do."

He shifted, aware people sometimes thought him standoffish because he didn't blab about his life. "Not much to tell."

"I doubt it, but I'll let it slide for now." The amusement in her eyes turned serious. "Nora's kind of like the oil used to loosen tightly closed hinges, but in her case, lips. Before you know it, she'll have gotten you to tell her your whole life story."

He pushed back the mounting irritation. "Assuming I want to tell her."

"It's sweet you think you have a choice." She tilted her head. Her bright hair swung around her face. "You might as well just face it now, you stand no chance against Nora."

"We'll see."

She grinned again. "Yes, we will."

Later in the evening, Ben sat at one of Nora's worktables, measuring the cutouts to the templates to make sure they were even. Once again, he noticed all the quilting tools were similar to his sporting equipment, each one necessary to get the job done right. He had to put his all into the making of this quilt or he'd lose the challenge.

After spending much of the day with Molly, he realized the quiet woman she portrayed around the office hid a woman with a warm sense of humor, along with her innate concern about people. Her determination to win the challenge impressed him. He needed to keep an eye out for her in the future.

"Getting the hang of it, Ben?"

He glanced up as Nora crossed the room to take a look at his progress. He'd made sure to take note of the colors and patterns he was using so Molly wouldn't razz him later. Thinking he would master an unknown skill in no time flat, therefore giving him an advantage over Molly, had been faulty logic. There had to be an art to quilting and given his time here, he'd figure it out.

"So, how long have you worked with Molly?" Nora asked.

"Six months."

"She is a joy to be around."

"Honestly, I wouldn't know. The first weeks I worked at Master's Publishing, I was out of the office on location. Even though I've only been there full-time for a few months now, it's just been this past week I've come to know her."

"Because of the challenge?"

"Yeah."

Nora went quiet for a few moments, then said, "Seems an odd way to get a promotion."

Ben grinned. "You haven't met our boss."

"Molly said he is a bit . . . different."

"He is, but he's also very successful. I want the promotion to get more involved with the company than I am so far."

"So you want to be invested, right?"

He continued cutting. "It's my plan."

Nora went quiet for a moment, toying with a pile of shapes Ben had set to the side of his work area. "Do you have family here in Tampa?"

Here came the digging Molly warned him about. He paused before deciding if he should humor her. If he wanted to become involved with people on a personal level, he had to open up sooner or later. Why not here, with a woman who reminded him of his mother? "No."

"Sounds like a story in your answer."

He never liked talking about his parents. They were gone and nothing would change the fact, but perhaps enough time had passed to be able to share stories about them without experiencing the crushing sense of loss.

"I'm sorry," Nora said. "Did I cross a line here?"

"I don't talk about my private life."

She chuckled. "You're in a woman's world now. I'm afraid it's what we do—talk about our lives."

He breathed out a put-upon sigh. "Molly warned me about the potential prying."

Nora patted his hand, her soft skin reminding him of happier times, when his mother would fuss over him. "You don't have to say a thing if you don't want to."

He sized-up Nora, with her kind eyes, creamy, yet line-aged face, and noted a sense of serenity about her. Here was a perfect opportunity for a connection. A start in alleviating his loneliness. He had to take the first step, but he'd been solo for so long, he didn't know how.

Nora removed her hand, but before she could walk away, he said, "I'm an orphan."

Her eyes went wide.

"Okay, it sounds dumb since I'm not a little kid anymore." He took a breath and started over. "My folks died when I was in college. Car accident. They were all the family I had, so imagine my shock when I found myself all alone."

"No other relatives?"

"An aunt who lived up north, but I didn't know her."

Nora pulled a stool to the table and sat. "So you struck out on your own?"

"I'd planned on getting my own place after college, but I wasn't ready." Ben swallowed. "I've always been drawn to activities keeping me on the move. When I was a kid, we traveled a lot. My parents loved to visit exciting places. Guess I caught the bug from them. Then after they died . . ." he paused. Why did his chest still ache after all these years? "I figured if I didn't stay in one place long enough, I wouldn't miss my old life. Or focus on my loss. Worked for a long time."

"Until now?"

"Yeah."

"You're seeking something different now?"

He stared out the window, noticing the sun had nearly set. The twilight sky had turned a deep blue. Along with his mood. He answered her question by saying, "I'm tired of being alone."

"You're never alone, you know. If you're a believing man, you know God will never leave you nor forsake you."

"I went to church when I was a kid. After my parents' deaths, I was pretty angry. Haven't set a foot in a church building since."

"Are you still angry?"

Was he? It had been so long ago.

"Not as much. Still miss them though."

"My William has been gone five years and not a day goes by I don't miss him." Tears glistened in her eyes. "The good thing is, I'll see him again one day. Same for you with your parents."

"I think it would require me believing."

"And do you?"

He thought for a moment. "I've been around the world. Seen crazy things defying explanation. I've been exposed to different religions, but in the back of my mind, I always believed in the Lord. Haven't acted on it, but had the sense of, yes, God is part of my life. I guess it counts, right?"

"I'd say so. Everyone has a different time for an ah-ha moment. It doesn't have to be a huge epiphany. Sometimes just knowing is enough."

"Staying in one place will make me get serious about my life."

"And the promotion is a start?"

He nodded.

"You do realize Molly isn't going to give in easily." Nora chuckled. "The girl can be stubborn when she wants something."

"I'm beginning to agree." And appreciate the fact Molly wouldn't make any part of the challenge easy on him. Could this explain his attraction to her?

"Good. Many people overlook her. They shouldn't."

Ben wondered who those people were and why they would overlook Molly. In the past few days, she'd been on his radar. Because of the challenge, sure, but also because she'd become a personal challenge to him. She might be all buttoned-up, but he'd seen her cheeks blush when their eyes met across a room or when he teased her. Her passion for quilting and taking care of other people made her someone worth getting to know. He was about to ask why other people overlooked Molly when Nora held up her hand.

"You'll find out," was all she said.

Turning back to the cloth cutouts, Ben realized he looked forward to the journey. Especially with Molly on board.

6

Are you sure this thing is safe?" Molly asked, eyeing the kayak lying on the grass beside the lakeside like an alligator snoozing in the sun. And just as dangerous.

Her brother chuckled. "Jed's been boating a long time. He'll teach you safety and basic handling."

"Yippee."

What had Mr. Masterson been thinking? Didn't he realize she had no desire to be an outdoorsy kind of girl? Or maybe he had, making the challenge more appealing to him. She tried to stop the flush of anger, but decided to just give in. Once she got over the anger, the supposed Henderson moxie would kick in and she'd master kayaking on her very first try.

Right. Just like Ben would fail on the quilting front.

"I've known Jed since high school. He's been in business for years."

Molly pushed her glasses up her nose for the tenth time. Slathered from head to toe in suntan lotion, her glasses were a collateral casualty of skin protection. She'd moved from the canopy of leafy trees and stood at the mercy of the late morning sunshine, waiting for the lesson to begin. Feeling exposed in an oversized T-shirt and baggy shorts, her toes pinched in brand new water shoes. A steady breeze grasped the loose hair escaping her ponytail, then stuck to her damp skin.

Nearby, gentle waves lapped against a creaking wooden dock jutting out over the sparkling water of the private lake. The bank of worn grass sloped down to the water. A perfect place to launch a kayak.

If she believed in alternative universes, Molly would have been certain she'd stepped into one.

Paul playfully tapped her shoulder.

"Ow."

"C'mon. I barely touched you. Lighten up, Sis."

"I don't know, Paul. This is iffy, even for me."

Before he could respond with another round of "sure you cans," Jed called to Paul from the office.

"Be right back."

Paul jogged up the slight incline to the small cabin serving as Jed's office. Molly stared down at the kayak she'd soon step into, wishing she were anywhere else.

She'd gotten a few hours of work on the Hearts Entwined quilt before meeting Paul. Not enough time to make her comfortable she'd finish in time for the Charity Expo. What was wrong with her? She'd never been poky while working on a deadline. If she had her way, she'd be ensconced in her air-conditioned apartment, curled up on her couch, stitching together quilt pieces to her heart's content. But then, her life hadn't always panned out the way she'd prayed.

Maybe God was showing her a new plan, because she never thought she'd team up with her brother. Even her father had been encouraging. When had that ever happened?

Never, as far as she could remember.

Molly hadn't spent much time with Paul growing up. By the time her parents had her convinced she needed to stay indoors, he'd gone on to master everything he put his mind to. Great for parental pride. Not so great for the sibling bitterness she began to harbor in her heart.

Once she confided in Nora, she began to deal with her feelings. By then, Paul had moved on with his life and she hadn't had a chance to fix things between them. Until her boss tossed a monkey wrench in her ordinary life.

No matter her parents' concerns on the subject of her kayaking, Molly would cherish the time with her brother. Funny, it took a crazy challenge against an exasperating man to get her to go after what she wanted.

She touched the kayak with the toe of her shoe. Could one little boat be all standing between her and the promotion? Scary thought.

And what if she failed and Ben got the promotion? How would she handle dealing with another person who didn't see what she had to offer? She didn't want to think about the very real possibility right now. She had to master the art of kayaking, even if it took every ounce of grit she possessed.

Blowing out a huge sigh, she whispered a quick prayer of safety just as Paul exited the office, carrying a big bag with his good arm, Jed in tow.

"Okay, Sis. Kayak time."

"I'm ready." *To get my first lesson over with.*

Paul waved her over, then pulled the string on the bag and reached inside to remove a helmet, life vest, and some other thing she didn't recognize.

"What's this?"

"A spray skirt," Jed explained. "You wear it to keep the splashing water from entering the boat, or if you happen to flip over, the boat won't fill with water."

Molly glanced at Paul, sure she had panic written on her face.

"Don't worry. You'll get the hang of it."

Jed smiled. "It's not a big deal. The spray skirt fits around your torso as well as the cockpit. Once you get used to it, you'll be fine."

Molly took a deep breath. "Okay."

She stepped into the skirt opening and Jed helped her roll it up over her clothes to her waist, followed by a part Jed called the tunnel. When he finished, Paul handed her the life vest. She slipped it on, pushing her brother's hands away when he tried to button it up for her.

"I think I can handle it."

He frowned.

She rolled her eyes at him. "Humor me."

Next, he took the helmet and plopped it on her head. She let him fasten it in place before moving it around, which of course squeezed her glasses to her head so they didn't fit right.

"Problem?" Paul asked, humor lacing his tone.

"Nope. Fine." No way would she complain, even if she had to continue with blurry vision. "And I don't need all your fussing."

"Sorry, little sister. Habit."

"Well, cut it out. I'm not a child anymore and I am more than capable of taking care of myself."

Paul saluted. "Yes, ma'am."

Jed pulled the kayak to the shallow water. Molly followed, still adjusting her glasses to a comfortable position.

"Now the kayak is in the water, so let's get you settled inside," Paul said in his take-charge tone.

"Just do it," Molly muttered under her breath. She walked to the water's edge, almost slipped on the mud, but caught herself. Paul reached out a hand and led her to the kayak, holding on as she stepped into the shallow water. He held the boat secure as she stepped into the cockpit and sat down. "Comfortable?"

She wiggled around. "Yes."

"Good. Now I want you to get out and get back in on your own."

She gaped up at him.

"Hey, you've got to learn, Molly. I won't always be around to help you."

Yeah, she knew.

"To get out, lean to one side and put your hand on the shore."

She did as he instructed.

"Good. Now, keep one foot in the boat and place the other on the ground, which will steady you and the boat."

She followed through, thrilled when she didn't land face first in the mud.

"Now, get back in."

She shuffled into the water, held the boat secure, and managed to get back in without too much fuss. Jed showed her how to attach the spray skirt and handed her a paddle. After detailed instruction and practice on paddle-stroking, Molly built up the confidence to paddle away from shore.

Paul called out tips as she eased away from the bank. At first, she flailed with the paddle, causing water to splash her face and spot her glasses. On the next pass by, she took them off and handed them to her grinning brother. Maybe she'd break down and get contacts like Taylor had been nagging her to do.

For the next hour she practiced. Back and forth. Forth and back, all the while Paul's steady voice giving her confidence. Soon she'd lost count of the laps she'd paddled. Her sore muscles twitched and the paddle weighed a ton. Her legs, achy from keeping them braced against the sides of the kayak for support, grew numb. Her skin went from pink to red from too much sun exposure. Please, she whined silently, let it be time to call it a day.

With her intense focus on the task at hand, Molly didn't realize she'd paddled so far from shore until Paul's voice faded. She glanced over her shoulder, squinting in the distance to see him waving like crazy. She wondered what was going on, until she heard the sound of an engine. Turning the other way, she watched a motorboat whizz by, creating a good-size wave in its wake.

Panic seized her. Would she flip over? What did she do now? *Calm down.*

She stopped, regrouped as she floated with the waves and tried to remember Paul's words. She maneuvered the paddle on one side, stroking through the water until she managed to steer the boat around. Breathing easier, she resumed the back and forth paddling motion until she glided to the shore.

"You made it," Paul yelled at her.

"Sure did," she yelled back.

She exited the boat without mishap, even with shaky legs. Paul, seeing her fatigue, gave her mercy and helped her remove the spray skirt, then handed her a cold water bottle. She took a long swig, grateful for the refreshing water after spending time in the hot sun. After recapping the bottle, she grabbed hold of the boat to tug it on shore. Wisely, Paul let her do it alone.

Her fingers, still wet, slid over the fiberglass and she lost her grip. The kayak slipped out of her hold and slammed into wet dirt. Mud flew up to cover her legs, arms, and the part of her face not covered by the helmet. She shook out her hands, flexed them to relieve the cramps, which had started with a vengeance after an hour of white-knuckling the paddle, and tried again. The next time she dragged the kayak to the grass.

Thankful to be on solid ground and in one piece, she removed her helmet with a flourish, excited she'd had a disaster-free first lesson. She ran a hand through her damp, unruly hair and retrieved her glasses from her brother. As she headed toward the cabin to clean up, she stopped dead in her tracks. Ben stood at the top of the incline. Dressed in worn jeans and T-shirt, hands tucked into his back pockets, a big smile curved his lips.

"How . . . what are you doing here?" she sputtered.

For an hour, she hadn't thought about him, the challenge or quilting. Her mind and body worked as one to keep her occupied. She hadn't thought about her job, or the fact she liked Ben enough to worry about what would happen to their working relationship once the challenge ended. One of them would end up with the job. One might hold a grudge.

Now it all came rushing back, as well as her feminine instinct to want to pull a bag over her head. Why did he have to show up when she looked like such a mess? Wet clothes covered by a soggy life vest. Splattered mud. Lovely.

Wait. "How did you know I was here?"

He jogged toward her with the answer. "Called your cell phone. Your brother answered."

She shot an exasperated glare at her brother. "My phone is in my purse, in the office."

"I went to get some water bottles." He shrugged, his full smile not conveying any semblance of guilt. "Sis, your phone rang three times in a row. Thought there might be an emergency, so I looked. When I saw Ben's name on the caller ID, figured it must be important. And it was. Ben needs to talk to you."

As if. More like he wanted to size up the competition. She frowned as she tried to gracefully remove the life vest. Her T-shirt rode up, giving Ben a glance at her stomach. She yanked the shirt down. No need to get even more personal than they already had.

Dropping the vest to the ground, she smoothed her hair. Nothing could save the tangled mess. "Checking up on me?"

"Kind of like you hovering over me at Nora's house."

"I didn't hover."

"No. You made sure I was in over my head."

True. "So we're even?"

He cocked his head as he took her in from head to toe. Shivers broke out over her sweltering skin. "Not by a long shot. I had a different reason for calling."

She forced herself to calm down as she waited for him to reveal the reason for his unexpected arrival. "Well?"

"Clean up. Mr. Masterson called. He wants to see us both. We have about thirty minutes to get downtown."

———

Ben hid his grin. Miss Molly didn't realize her cute factor when things weren't going her way. Between her stomping across the grass and the annoyed angle of her brows, she had a good head of steam going. If he could mess with her head with such ease, he'd have the challenge won in no time.

"A meeting?" she asked as they walked toward the small office where she'd stowed her purse. "Today?"

"Masterson has to go out of town so he requested a quick meeting with us. When he called me, he mentioned he couldn't get a hold of you and asked me to try."

"I didn't get a call."

Molly disappeared inside, leaving Ben standing outside with her brother. He held out his hand. "Ben Weaver."

"Paul Henderson." They shook hands. "Does your boss usually call meetings on Saturday? Molly seems a bit rattled."

"Not normally."

"And keeping Molly guessing is working to your advantage?"

"It's not hurting."

Paul scowled. "Listen, she's my little sister and I don't want to see her dreams crushed, so lighten up."

Ben lifted his hand. "Hey, I'm not messing with her on purpose. It's the boss's call."

Paul's lips formed a thin line. He needed more convincing Ben didn't have a personal vendetta against his sister.

"Look, I'm not out to hurt Molly, but I want the job just as much as she does. And for the record, I'd have picked a sport a little more suited for her strength, but I didn't have a say."

Paul's expression softened a small bit. "And just so you know, Molly's taken to kayaking quite well. She's not a quitter.

"So I'm finding out."

Surprise passed over Paul's face, followed by approval of Ben's appraisal of his sister. "Then be prepared, buddy."

Molly walked outside, purse strap over her shoulder, phone in one hand, a paper towel in the other as she distractedly wiped her face. "Three missed calls." She frowned. "Two from the office. One from you."

"See, no nefarious reason for showing up here."

Her guileless blue eyes shone behind her glasses. "I still don't know what Mr. Masterson would have to discuss with us."

"We now have about twenty minutes to find out."

She glanced down at her messy clothes. Panic crossed her sun-kissed face. "I can't go dressed like I just spent the day on the lake. It's not professional."

"I don't think you have enough time to go home to shower and change. Sounds like Masterson is on a tight schedule."

"Great, just great," she muttered as she dug in her purse for her car keys. "I'll see you there," she said as she stalked off.

"Remind me again how you think you're gonna win?" Paul asked as they watched his sister walk away.

"It's going to come down to who wants the job more."

Paul chuckled and held out his good hand for a farewell shake. "Good luck."

On the drive to the office, Ben wondered how Molly would handle the impromptu meeting with the boss in less than professional clothing. While he tended to push the envelope with his idea of casual work clothes, she always had a buttoned-up professional look he'd come to think of as her armor. Unless she had an entire closet of clean professional clothes in her car, which he doubted, she couldn't do much about the circumstances. She might be particular, but a car closet was way too much even for her.

When he parked and met Molly, he got his answer. She hurried toward the parking garage elevator wrapped up in a trench coat, buttoned from chin to knees.

"You're a spy now?"

"Ben, you're in Florida, remember?" she snapped. "A smart person keeps a rain coat in the car, just in case. You never know when a stray shower will hit."

He glanced down. "Shoes too?"

"I always keep an extra pair with me, for the same reason. I've gotten drenched in enough unexpected downpours to be prepared. You, of all people, should know you can't run off on an adventure without the right equipment."

"Since when does a rainstorm constitute an adventure?"

"Have you been away so long you've forgotten what the weather is like here? Just wait. As soon as summer rolls around and you get soaked without the necessary rain protection, I'll say I told you so."

He chuckled. He liked it when she told him off. Not many people did. Usually the people around him were trying to suck up in hopes he'd help advance their careers. Not Molly.

"Isn't it hot in your coat?" he messed with her.

"Hot or not, I'm not letting our employer see what's underneath."

Ben chuckled. He hadn't had this much fun in a long time.

They stepped out of the elevator on Masterson's floor. Molly grabbed his arm to stop him. She'd brushed her wavy hair on the way over and attempted to clean her face. "Do I look okay?"

More than okay. "Not like your usual put-together self, but fine."

"I don't like being caught off-guard."

"Yeah, I figured." He noticed a smudge of mud under her chin. "Do you mind?"

"What?"

He reached over to wipe it off.

Her cheeks turned pink. "Thanks."

"Hey, fellow competitors need to stick together."

They stood for a moment, smiling at each other until a voice broke the silence. "I've got ten minutes, people. Let's go."

Ben dropped his hand as if it had spontaneously combusted. Molly cleared her throat, pushing her glasses up the bridge of her nose. A nervous tell he'd come to recognize. When they reached the office their boss tossed files into an open briefcase on his desk. He glanced up as they entered.

"Sorry to get you both down here on your day off, but I've been called out of town unexpectedly and need to discuss a few things with you both." He nodded towards the chairs angled before his desk. "Have a seat."

As they sat, Ben noticed Masterson do a double-take at Molly's outfit, but if the man thought her choice a bit odd, he didn't say a word. Smart guy.

"I've had a personal matter come up," he said. "I'll be out of town for at least a week. So you know, everything is on target for the new magazine. I'll have some updates when I get back to town, but before I leave, I have another project I need you both on."

He closed his briefcase with a snap. "I'm scheduled to attend the Mayoral Achievement Awards next Saturday night, but since I'll be gone I'd like you both to go in my place. Think of it as the perfect opportunity to get face time in the community before I announce the new magazine and the editor-in-chief."

Masterson eyed them both. Ben didn't miss the unspoken admonition. Despite the challenge he'd issued, he expected the same level of professionalism as he himself would bring to the event.

"You know I like to be visible in the public eye, so I expect you to be my eyes and ears while I'm gone. Any questions? Comments?"

Ben couldn't think of a thing, except he didn't go to high-profile events. Not as if he'd offer up that bit of information, though. Jumping out of an airplane was one thing, schmoozing with people, a completely different skill set. But it wasn't a suggestion. He needed to put on his game face and attend. Interacting with strangers on a business level would help him expand his people skills, which he needed to do if he wanted to be part of the community, instead of remaining the loner he'd turned into.

Masterson stood and rounded his desk, two envelopes in his hands. He handed one to Molly, then Ben. "The invitations with all the information. I know I put the challenge into play, but I need team players at the ceremony. I expect your professionalism to be on display." He nodded in dismissal. "Now, if you'll excuse me, I need to make a few phone calls before I leave."

Ben followed Molly out of the office. They walked to the elevator in silence until they'd gotten out of hearing distance.

"He called us in on a Saturday for this?" Molly whispered as she pushed at her glasses. "His secretary couldn't have filled us in?"

"Apparently not." Ben tried not to chuckle as Molly grumbled under her breath. "Have you been to many award ceremonies?"

"We don't get invited because Mr. Masterson likes the spotlight, but I know this event is important to him. He's attended for the past five years, hoping to be awarded."

Ben frowned. "Hasn't received recognition yet?"

"No. He must not think he'll be mentioned or he'd arrange to be there. I can't imagine him not attending, otherwise."

Could it be as simple as that? While Masterson hadn't been as cagey about the event as he had about the challenge he'd issued, he'd worked with the boss long enough to know Masterson might have something up his sleeve. Could it be another way to see how he and Molly would handle the new job? Or just Ben's imagination? Could there be more behind them attending the event together? If he started trying to figure his boss out now, he'd never get any work done.

"Why do you think he's going to so much trouble?" Molly asked, a perplexed expression flitting across her face.

"Trouble?"

"You know, pitting us against each other, then throwing us together for a work event?"

"Wants to see how we handle pressure?"

Molly unbuttoned her raincoat. "It's like he can't make up his mind."

"You think there's more to it?"

"In all the years I've worked here, he's never had an excuse not to attend a publicity function. If he can be in the local spotlight, he'll make sure he removes all obstacles to get there."

"So he does have something up his sleeve."

"I can't be sure," Molly agreed, shrugging off the coat. "But I'd say so."

"Then I guess we'll have to give him what he wants," Ben said, a cocky smile tugging his lips. "Two exemplary employees representing Master's Publishing."

Molly narrowed her eyes at him. "Why do I get the feeling we're headed for trouble?"

"Oh, ye of little faith."

As she thought about it, he watched her frown turn into a grin. Uh-oh. What had he roused up in her?

"You know what? You're right. I'm going to be so professional, it'll be another step toward *me* getting the new editor position."

He liked her spunk. It lit up her face and almost . . . almost made him want to see her win the position, if only to glimpse the joy and excitement, as well the gloating, on her face. "Not going to happen, so enjoy the fun and games for now."

7

Wednesday rolled around before Molly made it to the eye doctor during her lunch hour, hoping to get a prescription for contacts. After her first kayaking lesson, she'd realized she'd have to bite the bullet, because water-spotted lenses didn't cut it. The doctor had suggested goggles over the contacts, but she already looked bad enough with the helmet. She wouldn't let Ben see her totally geeked out. She left his office with a prescription and a sample box of contacts.

Which brought her back to the recurring theme bugging her ever since she and Ben had become rivals. What did it matter what Ben thought about the way she looked? She shouldn't care, except she did. Thought about it every time they were together. Good grief. She had to stop dwelling on Ben and focus more on the job promotion, because if Ben won, there'd be no living with him.

To get off this train of thought, she sat at her desk, studying the box of contacts as if they could solve all her problems, when Taylor knocked on the door and walked in, catching Molly in the act.

"What have you got there?" she asked.

Molly hesitated before admitting, "Contacts."

"No way. You took my advice?"

"Not exactly." She explained the kayaking problem.

"Well, it's still a good idea. Your eyes are so pretty and you insist on hiding behind glasses."

Exactly why Molly wore glasses. She liked hiding behind frames. Removing the shield made her vulnerable. Exposed. Like everyone could see her for the fraud she believed herself to be. Silly, but if her parents never believed in her, why should anyone else?

She shook off the old wounds. "What's up, Taylor?"

"Just curious about the Hearts Entwined quilt. The art director wants to set up a time for the photographer to take pictures for the layout."

Molly blew out a breath. "I should have the top finished by next week."

"I thought you were shooting for this weekend."

"Something has come up to set my timetable back a bit longer."

"Like what?"

"The Mayoral Achievement Awards."

Taylor plopped down into a chair. "You're going?"

"Mr. Masterson had to go out of town, so he asked Ben and me to go in his place."

"Wow. He always goes to those functions himself." Taylor pondered the idea for a few moments before her eyes lit up. "What are you going to wear?"

"I have no idea." Molly chuckled. Leave it to Taylor to get right to the heart of the matter. Fashion. "I've been busy poring over the reader letters that came in with the fabric. Trying to decide which one to use."

"It's not like you to be so indecisive."

"I feel like each letter is deserving of a mention. There are a few standout stories, of course, but I feel like there should be more. The whole concept behind the heart quilt is to showcase the journeys of these women."

"This project has become personal to you, hasn't it?"

"Yeah. It has."

Molly glanced down at some of the letters scattered on her desk. Ever since coming up with the idea to include the readers in the making of the heart quilt, she felt more connected with her readers than ever before. How she wished she could meet every one of them, see their faces as they told their stories, hear the timbre of their voices as they spoke. A bond had formed. It wasn't just about quilting, but more about the people behind the quilt. Could she do these women justice in the next issue? With the finished quilt? She wanted to make the women who had taken a chance on sending in their stories proud of the way she handled each and every one. And while she'd always had enough content to fill each magazine, it seemed she had more words than usual to fill a dozen magazines or more. Why was she having such a hard time getting started?

For the first time she found herself floundering as an editor. If she couldn't pull the next issue together, what made her think she could handle being editor-in-chief?

"You still have a few days before the awards," Taylor said. "What do you say we go shopping for a new dress. The spring lines are out. We can find you something drool-worthy to wear."

She nearly laughed out loud. Drool-worthy? As opposed to her unassuming fashion sense?

"You deserve it, Molly."

Did she? She glanced at the letters again. She should take notes from the women who sent in their stories. Stories of courage and love. Understanding and healing. Acceptance. If these women could make it through hard times and experience the joy of life, couldn't she?

"I'll tell you what. Give me a few hours to decide what to do with the next magazine issue and we can hit the mall."

Taylor jumped up. "You won't regret it."

"I already am."

As Taylor danced out of the office, Molly rose to cross the small room to retrieve her tote bag. She pulled out the nearly completed quilt top and spread it out over the surface of the table to admire her work. The heart shapes were recognizable now. Next came adding the border. It shouldn't take too long, but she'd spent too much time pondering each piece of fabric, remembering the story with each scrap. It had added days to the project.

Nora always said a part of you went into each project. Each quilt a labor of love. Her quilt certainly qualified.

From the moment the idea had popped into her mind, she'd been more engrossed than in any other project. As she thought back, she remembered the idea had come when she'd returned from a day of volunteering at Second Chances.

It had been a Saturday. She'd planned to have breakfast with her parents, but her father called last minute to cancel. She didn't ask why, didn't care to know. Besides, they'd cancelled on her so many times before, she should have been used to it.

Bummed, she arrived early at Second Chances. She'd gotten to work cleaning the kitchen and the common room. Once she had a bag filled with trash, she opened the back door, stumbling over a lump on the step as she carried the bag to the Dumpster.

The lump turned out to be a young woman bundled up in a blanket. Once Molly caught herself from falling, she came face to face with a panic-stricken girl.

"I'm sorry," the girl said as she jumped, hastily rolling up the blanket. "I know I shouldn't be here."

Molly placed a firm hand on the girl's shoulder to keep her from taking off. "It's ok. You're more than welcome to come in. I made a fresh pot of coffee. I'm sure I can rustle you up some breakfast."

The girl hugged the blanket to her chest. "I don't know. I don't want to be a burden." She paused and said just above a whisper, "I don't have anywhere else to go."

How many times had Molly heard this same statement? Too many to count. Women came to the center scared and needing help, but felt guilty about it. Or unworthy. Molly's heart melted every time she assured one of the women they could stay here, no questions asked.

"My name is Molly. What's yours?"

"Trish."

"Okay then, Trish, how about I fix you breakfast if you promise to clean up afterward."

The girl hesitated, but a hopeful light flickered in her eyes. "I can help."

Molly tossed the bag in the Dumpster then said, "Follow me."

Trish took a few steps and sagged, resting against the side of the building. Molly rushed to her side. "Are you okay?"

"Just a little lightheaded."

"I'm guessing you haven't eaten lately?"

Trish's face turned red and she lowered her head.

"I thought so." Wrapping her arm around Trish's waist, Molly led her inside to the common room just beyond the kitchen and helped her take a seat at the dining table.

"I'll be right back."

Molly hustled into the kitchen to pour a glass of orange juice, then back to hand it to Trish. "Here you go. Just sip, okay? Don't want to upset your stomach."

Trish eyed the glass, then Molly and took a sip.

"Now, would you prefer eggs or oatmeal?"

Trish took another sip. "Whatever is easiest."

Molly grinned. "I'll surprise you."

Knowing there were two families staying at the shelter and they'd be coming over for breakfast soon, Molly pulled a carton of eggs and bread from the refrigerator and got the meal started. She even made oatmeal, thinking she'd encourage Trish to fill her belly.

Humming, she scrambled the eggs and stirred the oatmeal.

"What can I do?"

Molly jumped as she whirled around to find Trish standing in the middle of the kitchen, looking sad and lost. "You startled me."

"Sorry." Trish stuffed her fingers in her jeans pockets.

"Are you feeling better?" Molly asked over her shoulder, as she turned back to the food.

"Yes, thanks."

"Then how about you start the toast."

They worked in silence for a few minutes. She'd wanted to give Trish time to feel comfortable before making conversation.

"Do you live around here?"

"No."

"Left home?"

Trish kept her head down. "Yes."

"Good idea?"

Trish's head shot up. "Why would you ask?"

Molly shrugged. "Lots of times we make decisions because we think the grass is greener elsewhere. You're rather young to be alone."

"I didn't get along with my parents. Decided to make it on my own."

"And?"

"It hasn't worked out too well."

Once the eggs were finished, Molly turned off the stove, scooping the eggs onto a plate and the oatmeal into a bowl. She placed the pan in the sink before wrapping an arm around Trish's shoulders and spoke to her from the heart. "Just because you left home and things didn't work out doesn't mean you don't deserve a second chance. Life is all about making decisions and living with the consequences. You can keep making mistakes or you can take those experiences and change your life. It's up to you."

"You don't understand. My parents won't take me back."

Oh, Molly understood. Her parents hadn't forced her to leave home, but she'd never had the sense of belonging. She'd had her church family to keep her out of trouble. Hopefully, she could encourage Trish the same way.

"When was the last time you spoke to them?"

"Six months ago."

"What did they say?"

"I should stop being foolish and come home."

Okay, not the best choice of words, but she'd learned since working here, in times of extreme emotional duress, wrong words were often spoken. "So you decided to stay away?"

"No. After I got off the phone, I went to the bus station. I met a guy." Her face colored again. "We got to talking and he bought me lunch. He was sweet and nice to me. The next thing I knew, I missed the bus and decided to stay with him."

"So how did you end up out back?"

"He turned kind of mean. I got scared and left. Without any money, I've been living on the street, trying to figure out what to do. Some lady told me about this place and I came by last night. I just couldn't work up the nerve to knock on the door."

Molly gave her a quick hug. "You're here now and you're safe. If you want to go home, we can help you."

Tears brimming in Trish's wide eyes. "You'd do that for me?"

"You bet." Molly grabbed a tissue and wiped away the tears on Trish's cheek. Her heart ached for the precious girl who needed her family. "You bet."

Trish had gone home and started over. For every success story, there were plenty more women who went back to the streets or other abusive relationships. As long as there were women who needed help, Molly would continue to work at the center, to try and make a difference. To encourage and build up self-esteem. To assure them they, indeed, had a second chance if they wanted it.

Molly ran her fingers over the material again, remembering why this project touched her so deeply. When she worked at the center, she became a different person. Not the disappointment to her parents, but a hopeful voice to women who needed hope. And didn't she want to give her readers hope, too? *Quilters Heart* may be a magazine about quilting, but it would also be an encouraging magazine.

She dug into the tote again, removing a frayed, faded pink baby blanket she'd held onto all these years. She'd been struggling with the idea of adding her own piece of fabric to the quilt. Didn't she have her own story to tell? The story of how her passion for quilting had come at a time when loneliness consumed her life to the point of pain. How passion moved her from pain to promise. If she added her bit of fabric to the quilt, she joined a sisterhood of women who grabbed hold of their promise.

She took the scissors and cut the blanket into four separate squares. She would incorporate the shapes into the corners of the border. Once she completed the task, a thought occurred to her.

She snipped another piece of the baby blanket. Folding it to fit in the palm of her hand, she left her office, walking nonchalantly to the elevator. Once inside she pressed the button to move up one floor.

Once there, she scanned the hallway, breathing in relief. No one in sight. With a brisk pace, she hurried to the empty office she and Ben had been enticed with last week. She eased open the door, peeked her head inside. Empty. She rushed in, closing the door behind her with a gentle nudge.

Oh, how she loved the open space and huge windows. Such a breath of fresh air after her small, cramped office. If she had her way, she'd move the desk close to the natural light and bask in it every day.

On the desk sat Ben's baseball. Curious, she picked up the cool, clear plastic, peering at the memento stored inside. She could just make out the scratchy handwriting on the dirty, worn ball. Obviously a childhood treasure of Ben's. Just like her blanket.

She grinned. Why hadn't she thought to bring something of hers up here before today? If Ben could leave a baseball, she'd leave a piece of her blanket. It would make them even. In her mind, anyway. Pleased with her decision, she laid the blanket piece on the opposite side of the desk. In her mind's eye, she imagined them on either side of the desk, palms down, leaning forward as they squared off. Mr. Masterson's challenge notwithstanding, she could hold her own with Ben. She enjoyed their verbal sparring enough not to worry about the consequences. Enough to look forward to the next time they met in the ring, so to speak.

Satisfied with her covert mission, she turned on her heel, intending to get back to work. Until her gaze tangled with amused brown eyes.

"You got some 'splainin' to do, Molly," he said in his best Ricky Ricardo voice.

Busted.

Ignoring the heat creeping up her neck, she countered, "How did you know I was here?"

"You aren't very stealthy."

"I wasn't trying to be."

He pushed from the door frame and sauntered into the room. "I saw you leaving the office. You had an odd look on your face, so I followed. Watched the elevator light stop one floor up." He shrugged. "Thought you might be up to no good. Was I right?"

"Are you always so suspicious?"

"When it comes to the challenge." He walked to the desk and picked up the fabric. "Baby blanket?"

"From when I was a kid." She pointed to the baseball. "You left your mark. I left mine."

"We've both staked our claim. I get it."

Molly picked up the ball. "Who signed it?"

"Cal Ripken Jr. Only the greatest."

"I have no clue."

He chuckled as he took the box from her hand. His fingers brushed over hers and shivers shot up her arm. "That's what I like about you. You don't put on airs."

"Also makes me a good opponent."

"Good point."

"So, what's the story behind the ball?"

His good humor faded. "My dad caught it. It was the last game we went to together."

"Because . . .?"

He stared at the ball, silent for a long moment. Had she hit a nerve?

"My folks were in a fatal car accident about six weeks later."

Her stomach dropped. How could she have been so thoughtless? "Oh Ben. I'm sorry."

He shrugged. She imagined his casual response covered a deep hurt.

"How long ago?"

"When I was in college."

She couldn't even imagine. Despite the strained relationship with her parents, at least she knew they were around. Who did Ben have?

"Any brother or sisters?"

"Nope. Just me."

Even worse. "My goodness. How did you cope?"

He wandered to the window to stare at the scene below. "Went on the road and never came back."

His actions sure explained a lot. Like why he had the reputation as a loner. Why it had taken him so long to settle down in one place.

She wanted to reach out. Smooth the frown wrinkling his brow. Soothe the hurt tearing up his heart. She curled her fingers tight, because she somehow knew Ben wouldn't appreciate her pity.

"If you ever want to—"

He turned, his voice gruff when he said, "I'm good."

No need to press the issue. His closed expression screamed, "Do Not Trespass."

"Then I guess we're finished here."

"Just so we're on the same page here," he nodded to the blanket piece, "this battle isn't over."

"I never said it was."

"Good." His gaze caught hers. She didn't bother denying the flush of excitement. The shimmer of awareness arcing between them should have been cause for concern, but instead of shying away, Molly smiled into the face of her rival.

8

Saturday evening, Molly stood in the lobby of the Grand Hyatt Tampa Bay, gazing at her surroundings. The French-vanilla-colored walls, cream couches and chairs with amethyst accents, and French provincial furniture created an air of elegance. The scent of freshly cut flowers greeted guests as they walked through the grand doors. A sweeping stairway added a touch of drama. Marble floors shone under sparkling chandeliers. Voices echoed as people milled around the lobby.

As she waited for Ben, she adjusted the hand-embroidered shawl flowing over her new dress. Taylor had convinced her to do a complete head-to-toe makeover and she couldn't wait to see his response.

A few days before, she'd tried on dozens of dresses before settling on a sleeveless floral in bright pinks, yellows, and greens with a fitted bodice and skirt flaring out around her knees. Next, they'd found a pair of strappy sandals and small purse to finish the ensemble. Fun, flirty, and so unMollylike, yet she couldn't help but feel like a princess at the ball. She liked the new, different feeling.

After shopping, Taylor surprised Molly by arranging to have her hair styled along with an impromptu makeup lesson.

For tonight's outing, she'd managed to blow dry her hair to a close version of what the stylist had created, smoothing the usual unmanageable waves into a long wispy style framing her face. Her makeup had turned out okay, considering her face had been exposed to too much sun during her morning kayaking lesson.

Today, she'd had no major problems on the lake and had ventured farther from the shore than the prior lesson. She'd forgotten all about her fair skin until she pulled the kayak to shore where Paul informed her, tongue-in-cheek, she looked like a tomato.

As soon as she got home she'd showered and slathered on a gallon of lotion, but couldn't tone down the redness. Her skin had pinched from the sunburn, but standing here in the air-conditioned lobby, she purred in relief.

Scanning the room again, she reached up to push her glasses higher on her nose, only to touch skin. She'd debated between wearing her contacts or glasses tonight, then threw caution to the wind. If she was going to be the belle of the ball, why not look the part? So here she stood. New dress. New look. New Molly?

Glancing at her watch again, she decided to give Ben five more minutes when she heard, "Molly?"

She swung around, the skirt flaring out about her legs, and came face-to-face with Ben and his incredulous expression.

"Yes, it's me. Who else would it be?"

He swallowed, clearly tongue-tied. Was this good or bad? His gaze roamed from her styled hair to her snazzy shoes, then back to her face. It took everything in her to not to pull the wrap tighter and cover her new dress. She breathed, letting her muscles relax to enjoy the very poleaxed male expression staring at her.

"Earth to Ben. We have about fifteen minutes to get to the ballroom."

"Yeah." He looked her over again. "Right."

She bit back a grin. "Is something wrong?"

"You."

She placed a hand over her heart, pretending surprise. "Me?"

He frowned. "I didn't mean it the way it sounded. You just look so different."

"Different from what?" She couldn't help it, she had to yank his chain.

"From work, I guess." He tilted his head. "What is it?"

Before he dissected her appearance any further, she glanced at her watch. "I don't know, but let's get going before we're late."

Ben fell in step beside her and she snuck a sideways glance. Tonight he'd dressed in a charcoal suit with a pale blue shirt and patterned tie. His shoes shone in the overhead light. His short brown hair gleamed in the same lighting, his skin healthy, his face handsome.

Walking next to him, she straightened her shoulders and held her head high. Wondering what the night would be like if they were on a date. A real date. Nothing as mundane as a work function or the manufactured challenge by the boss, but a real, true date where Ben asked her out because he wanted to.

Molly would have loved to tuck her hand in the crook of Ben's arm. To feel the strength of his arms under the rich cut of the suit. They'd stand close, shoulder to shoulder and her heart would race, just as it did this moment in time. She'd daydreamed about Ben far too often to be smart, especially since he didn't act like anything more than a coworker. A rival coworker, at that. Oh sure, there'd been a few and far between moments when they'd caught each other's eye and couldn't seem to break the connection. Judging by his reaction to her new look, she wondered if he might be just a bit interested in her. And if so, what would she do if he acted on her fantasy?

Shaking off her fanciful thoughts, she opened her clutch purse to remove her invitation as they entered the ballroom. Ben pulled his from the inside pocket of his tailored jacket.

They entered the room, already filled with mingling guests. The plush carpets muted conversation. Shimmery, pearl-colored cloths covered the tables. A beautiful arrangement of red and purple orchids, lavender hydrangeas, and cream roses dominated the center.

Ben took hold of her elbow as he navigated the way to their seats. His touch made her shiver in delight.

"Cold?"

"No. I mean, yes."

"Which one is it?" he asked, humor lacing his tone.

She moved away to tug at the shawl slipping down her arms. When they reached the table, she set down her bag. "We should socialize."

Ben continued to stare at her. "Um, socialize. Right."

"What is wrong with you?"

"I can't get over . . . wait. Where are your glasses?"

"At home."

He frowned. "Then how—"

"Contacts."

"Right." He shook his head, as if coming back to his senses. "Right," he said, his voice more in control.

Molly decided right then female power ruled.

"Mingle?" she reminded him.

He nodded. "You go left, I'll go right."

She'd made a half-circuit of the room when she ran into an old friend. "Sarah?"

"Molly. So good to see you."

Sarah Lowery served as the head of the Charity Expo. Molly wasn't surprised to run into her here since her husband, a town councilman, attended these functions, placing Sarah in the strategic position of promoting the Expo at every public event she attended.

The Expo had been Sarah's brainchild. She'd started the project five years ago, pulling strings and calling in favors ever since. It had been a success every year, still going strong and helping many charitable organizations.

"What are you doing here?"

"Filling in for my employer," Molly explained.

"Right, Master's Publishing. I'm surprised Blake isn't here."

"He had to go out of town."

"Surprising. He never misses an opportunity to make headlines."

"True. So tell me, how are preparations for the Expo coming?"

"Right on schedule." Sarah filled Molly in on the details. "And how about the fabulous quilt I've been hearing about?"

Not on schedule, Molly thought, but kept the information to herself.

"You're about due for another award, Molly."

"You know I don't do it for accolades."

"No, but accolades get the word out."

Maybe, but the whole idea made Molly uncomfortable.

"Once I get the professional photos for the quilt, I'll send them to you."

"Thanks. Believe it or not, tying the quilt into a magazine article has created a buzz. People are already asking about it."

Which meant more donations. "I'm glad to hear it."

"Less than three weeks, my dear. Can't wait." Sarah started to walk away, then stopped, turned and faced Molly. "I almost forgot. I took the liberty of making up a poster for the Expo including the details about the quilt and its tie to your magazine. Hope you don't mind."

What could she say? No? Her magazine could use the extra marketing. Mr. Masterson would love the publicity.

Molly smiled as Sarah walked away, the weight of the magazine issue and the success of the quilt resting on her shoulders. She needed to work hard on so many different levels it gave her a headache. Of course, she could attribute the dull ache to staying out in the sun too long today. Or having to deal with Ben. Either one worked.

She continued roaming the ballroom, pleased to see one of the volunteers from Second Chances standing off to the side talking on her cell phone. Molly walked in her direction, reaching the woman as she ended the call.

"Molly. I'm so glad you're here."

As she drew closer, she noticed the distress on the other woman's face. "Linda, what's wrong?"

"I just got off the phone with my husband. Donny fell off the swing set. He might have broken his arm. My husband took him to the ER. I'm going to meet them there now."

Molly reached out to touch Linda's arm. "I'm so sorry."

"There's another problem." Linda pressed her lips together in disapproval. "Tammi isn't here."

Tammi Grayson, director of Second Chances, took over the job six months ago. In her short tenure, she'd missed meetings, both with the staff and volunteers, as well as community leaders. Molly filling in for her with the contractor was only one of the times she'd stepped in to help the organization.

"She's supposed to be here tonight," Linda continued. "You know the awards are a surprise, but the mayor's office invites the recipients in advance to make sure they'll be here if acknowledged. Tammi stood us up. Again."

Molly's heart sank. Second Chances had a good, solid reputation in the community. If Tammi continued down this path, she might destroy years of goodwill that past directors and volunteers had established.

"Molly, since you're here, would you mind stepping up if the mayor calls Second Chances?"

How could Molly say no? She didn't want to keep Linda from her son, and she didn't want to let Second Chances down.

"Go. I'll handle it."

Linda gave Molly a quick hug. "Thanks."

"And I'll be praying for your son."

After Linda took off, Molly finished circling the ballroom, afraid to run into anyone else who might need something else from her tonight.

She returned to their table. The air conditioning, which seemed like it had been set on freezing level, chilled her sunburned skin. She took a seat, wrapping the shawl over her shoulders.

"Too much sun?" Ben asked when he returned, pulling out the chair next to her to take a seat.

"Yes. And I'll end up with freckles before the challenge is over."

"I like freckles."

"And I like the indoors."

He chuckled. "The things we do to get ahead."

"Speaking of which, how's the quilting going?"

He held up red fingertips.

"Oh, dear."

"Nora couldn't find a thimble big enough to fit my finger."

"I'd say I feel sorry for you, but . . ." she pointed to her red nose.

Ben rubbed his fingertips together. "I'm wondering if the pain will be worth it in the end."

"Not when you lose."

He grinned. His face lit up and once again, Molly wondered what if. "Funny, coming from the woman who doesn't tan."

"Hey, Nature Boy, at least I'm not complaining."

He arched an eyebrow.

Oops. Now she'd done it. "Sorry. Office nickname for you."

"And here I thought everyone liked me."

"I don't think it's a matter of popularity. More your calling."

"Not after I win."

She had another retort on her tongue when the emcee tapped the live microphone.

"We're happy to see such a large turnout tonight. The mayor has all kinds of surprises in store, so settle back."

As the lights dimmed, Molly leaned toward Ben, catching a whiff of his very masculine cologne. "I forgot to tell you, I found out the mayor invites all the potential candidates for his awards without letting on who will win."

"Then why did Masterson ask us to attend?"

"He's been invited five years in a row and never got a mention. Must have figured this year would be another bust."

"And now," the emcee announced, "here is your mayor!"

Molly clapped along with the crowd, wishing she'd worn something a bit warmer than the sleeveless dress. She hugged herself against another round of chills. After a slight hesitation, Ben scooted his chair closer, draping his arm over her shoulders.

Everything inside Molly went still. She almost forgot to breathe. He'd gone out of his way to touch her tonight. Twice. Should she read anything into the gentlemanly gesture? She wanted to, oh, how she wanted to. But what if she misread Ben's intentions? His concern over her welfare might be the same for any woman.

As she got to know him better, she realized he was a nice guy. A guy any normal, red-blooded woman would love to date. The thought didn't make her feel better.

She arched a questioning brow at him.

"You're cold, right?"

"Yes, but—"

"Just until you warm up."

Oh, Molly had warmed up all right, if the blistering heat from her face gave any indication. How many times had she daydreamed about a scenario exactly like this? Just the two of them in a romantic setting? Too many to count since Ben started working for Master's Publishing.

She'd denied her growing feelings for Ben for too long now. Since they'd been working together, she'd been a bundle of confusion. She liked Ben. Okay, if she were honest with herself, more than liked. Admired his dedication. His playing along with Masterson's challenge to get the promotion. Plain and simple, a great guy. But deep inside, she couldn't help wondering if his attention tonight had anything to do with the challenge. Could he ever be interested in her?

She had no idea and was afraid to find out.

The mayor droned on for ten minutes before getting to the awards. He started off by announcing he had one particular organization he wanted to recognize before the others.

"For outstanding work in training victims of domestic abuse to get back into the workforce, our first award goes to Second Chances."

Molly clapped like crazy, until she noticed the mayor scanning the crowd. "Oh, I'll be back." She hurried to the dais, climbing the few steps to greet the mayor.

"Please, say a few words," he said.

In her moment of excitement, she hadn't considered the possibility of having to speak. Yikes.

Panic tightened her chest as Molly took a step toward the mic. The mayor cleared his throat. Molly swallowed hard and squeezed the triangular, heavy crystal award. She glanced down to read the engraved name, date of the event, and the organization, and her trepidation of speaking to the crowd diminished as her heart swelled with pride.

"I've been involved with Second Chances for over a year now. The women who have come through the doors have been an inspiration and a testament to the resilience of the human spirit. Second Chances opens the doors for women who desperately need a place to stay and gives them the skills and confidence they need to get back into the workforce to make a better life for themselves. On behalf of the board of directors, volunteers, and the women who seek us out, thank you."

A round of applause thundered in the room as she made her way back to the table.

"Something you forgot to tell me?" Ben muttered as she sat down, his jaw tight.

"Sorry. I found out earlier the director was a no-show and was asked to fill in."

He nodded, his tone genuine when he said, "Nice speech."

She swallowed hard. "Thanks."

The next thirty minutes brought other recipients to the dais to accept the awards until the mayor came to business recognition.

"It's always difficult to pick one business to honor each year because we have so many worthy business owners who give Tampa a good name. Our next recipient has a thriving business located here in our town and proudly calls Tampa his home. He's a man not afraid to shy from the limelight, so tonight we honor Blake Masterson for his work in keeping Tampa in the forefront of the media."

Molly's gaze flew to Ben's face. She imagined his shocked expression mirrored hers. Since they hadn't talked about going up front to accept the award, they both stood.

"Really?" he said in a low voice. "You've already been there once."

"Mr. Masterson asked us both to attend. It's only fair we accept together."

"Blake?" the mayor called out to the crowd.

"Fine, but I'll do the speaking," Ben said as they weaved through the tables.

"Fine," she shot back.

Once standing on the dais, the mayor handed Molly the award. She couldn't hide her satisfied grin as Ben glared at her.

Ben moved to the microphone, put on his charming face and gave the mayor thumbs up.

"Wow," he said into the mic. "The one year Mr. Masterson goes out of town and you surprise him. I have to say, he is going to be disappointed he missed tonight's ceremony." He nodded to the award.

"My esteemed colleague and I want to thank you, Mr. Mayor, for your generous award. We accept on behalf of Master's Publishing."

The crowd clapped.

"And one more thing. You'll know when Mr. Masterson gets back to town. I'm sure he'll have a special thank-you lined up. He's going to make sure you hear how much he regretted not being here tonight."

The crowd laughed as the mayor shook Ben's hand and spoke into the mic. "Trust me, Blake will let me know how he feels. Just how he does will be a surprise."

The mayor shook Molly's hand again. As she walked back to the table, the mayor announced the ceremony over and encouraged the guests to mingle. The lights came up, shining on the two awards placed on the table.

"Mr. Masterson is going to be upset he missed his two minutes on stage."

Ben chuckled. "You know our boss. He'll make up for it."

Molly gathered her clutch and shawl, along with the award for Second Chances. She gazed down at it, her heart full of joy. When she looked up, she found Ben staring at her, his eyes dark as he focused solely on her. She shivered again.

"Second Chances getting a mention means a lot to you."

"I've never been one to be all about awards and public recognition, but for the center, yes, it means a lot."

"Said the woman with all kinds of quilting awards."

How could she explain the impact Second Chances had on her life? "Those are different. I've never thought of awards as meaning I'm something special. The quilts are a way to raise money for organizations." She glanced down at the award again. "A way to make a difference."

"The most important part to you."

She stared at him again, her heart melting at his crooked grin. "Yes. Yes, it is."

9

It didn't take two seconds after Ben opened the door to his office Monday morning to realize someone had reconnected the speaker he'd disabled. "Ben's the man," blared from the loudspeaker. With every intention of taking care of the problem, he dropped his brief-case on a chair and strode to the door, bumping into his assistant as Charlie, face red and eyes wild, burst through the open doorway.

"I thought I disconnected this thing," Ben said, backing away from his harried assistant. "The loudspeaker has to go."

"We have more serious problems."

"As in?"

"Molly."

Yeah, Molly was a problem all right, but not the way Charlie thought.

When Ben had gotten a glimpse of her decked out at the award ceremony Saturday night, he had to blink a few times to make sure the vision before him was his usually buttoned-up coworker. He'd been searching for her when all along she'd been a few feet away, decked out in a colorful dress that brightened her face. He went from stunned to his heart rate ratcheting up a good ten degrees. The missing glasses threw him. Why now, when they were competitors, did she make a transformation right before his eyes? He wanted to keep her from winning the challenge, not think about kissing her senseless.

Her soft, sun-kissed skin tucked into her sassy outfit had him tangled up in more knots than usual. When she accepted the award for Second Chances, her bright smile captivated him as never before. He couldn't ignore the warmth in his chest. Later, sharing the stage with her for Master's Publishing had been perfect. Just perfect.

"She's all over the newspaper." Charlie's rant pulled Ben back to the present. Holding up the Sunday edition, his assistant asked, "What happened at the award thing?"

"Mr. Masterson got an award."

"It looks more like Molly did. Two of them."

"Technically, she accepted the awards on behalf of the winners."

"Still, she's the one in the paper. What about you?"

Charlie thrust the paper at Ben. He already knew what he'd find. No pictures of him, only a half-sentence mention of his name and job at Master's Publishing, while Miss Molly got all the attention.

"What is Masterson going to think?"

"We did what he asked. We showed up at the ceremony and represented Master's Publishing."

"Not good, Ben. He's going to see Molly's press and think she should get the promotion."

Ben had already thought about that. All day Sunday and into today. But the challenge was about the job, how Molly and Ben handled the tasks given to them. He considered the ceremony a slight setback, one he'd make up for.

"Charlie, calm down. I have things under control."

"You sure?" Charlie eyed Ben like he didn't quite believe him.

"I'm making progress on the quilt." He glanced down at his sore fingertips. "Well, as much as I can, but once I'm finished, I'm going to make sure I donate it to the Charity Expo Molly is involved in. When I make a big splash, Masterson will be impressed."

Charlie frowned. "I don't know."

"Look, I'm going to intrude on her territory and use it to my advantage. She won't be able to do the same."

"True. The kayak trip won't be easy for her."

"Stop worrying." He should listen to his own advice here. So far, Molly proved to be a formidable opponent. He needed to up his game if he wanted to impress Masterson. Which meant he had paperwork to catch up on. "Did you get the Tampa Bay Rays photographs I asked for?"

"Hmm, oh yeah," Charlie said in a distracted tone. "The PR department called. You need to set up a time for a team interview."

Ben brightened. "See, things are looking up. Masterson will like the media attention."

"Yeah. I've got to get on the layout."

"Hey, Charlie?"

The younger man turned.

"Thanks for looking out for me."

"Anytime."

Ben couldn't remember a time when someone had his back. He'd kept to himself so long, he never needed anyone or anything. Or so he thought. Now, getting settled here at the office and making a life for himself, he found making friends wasn't as hard as he'd expected. Sure, he hadn't wanted to put himself out there, but what had he gotten in return? Attending sporting events alone without good buddies to hang out with. Dinners solo. Sure, he dated, but he'd never connected with a woman he wanted to spend time with.

Especially after Cassie.

She'd been his high-school sweetheart. Stood beside him in those dark days after his parents' deaths. He'd cried his heart out to her, allowed her to see the deep, wrenching pain he would never reveal to anyone else.

Even though she'd been just a young woman, he realized now, she'd been ambitious. She'd sent headshots to a well-known modeling agency. They'd wooed her with the promise of fame and fortune. Tears rolling down his cheeks, he begged her to stay. Without looking back, she chose to pursue her dreams instead of staying with him.

When she walked out the door, he'd never cried again. Swore he'd never let his true feelings show, only to have them thrown back in his face. Adapted the attitude being strong meant he would never lose his self-control.

His parents' deaths may have partly closed the door on his emotions, but Cassie's leaving slammed the door shut.

He'd never gotten close to anyone since then. Hadn't considered what his isolation cost him. Until a woman he'd dated told him he was emotionally stunted. It stung, mostly because she spoke the truth.

He wondered what Molly thought about him. If those perceptive eyes saw more than she let on. Why did he have to be attracted to her? Now, under these circumstances? Figures. The more she got under his skin, the more he had to remind himself he couldn't let her keep him from getting what he wanted. No, what he needed. The chance to reconnect to the old Ben. So the more he dug his heels in, the better the outcome. As much as he liked Molly, he had to remember the goal here.

<hr />

"You're all over the newspaper!" Taylor greeted Molly as she stepped from the elevator into the lobby. "Do you have any idea what this publicity will do for your part in the challenge? You know how much Mr. Masterson loves the company name mentioned in the paper."

"And Ben and I made the company look good, if I do say so myself."

Molly contained a smug smile. Ben may have accepted the award, but she had her picture taken. Twice. If the boss didn't notice her now, she couldn't imagine what else she could do short of dancing on his desk proclaiming he'd be crazy not to pick her. Editing, okaying layout, production, and conducting team meetings would be a breath of fresh air in the aftermath of what she'd accomplished so far.

Office with the big windows, here I come.

"Problem is, you're still behind on the next issue of *Quilter's Heart*. You rescheduled the photo shoot once already. The art director wants access by early next week, so we don't fall behind. Think you can fit us all in?"

All the publicity in the world wouldn't impress her boss if she failed to deliver.

"Yes. Tell him Monday, for sure."

"And the article?"

"I looked over the letters you picked out," Molly said, as they entered her office. "We're on the same page with the content. I know I said we'd sit down and go over them, but I know where I want to focus the story now. I shouldn't have any problem making the deadline."

"Spoken by the Molly I know and love." Taylor pointed to the worktable where the still-unfinished quilt lay. "Don't let Ben get in your head."

Too late to stop him.

To be honest, it wasn't just Ben. Sure, he didn't help, since her mind always seemed to conjure visions of him when she least expected it. With the award ceremony, working at the center, and now having to meet her team of kayakers, she'd lost focus on her duties. Not good. She had to be able to handle all her commitments and more, if she expected to be an efficient editor-in-chief.

Molly stepped to the worktable, taking a moment to study the quilt. The time had come to leave the past behind and leap into a very bright future. She had a lot to offer this company in the years to come if Mr. Masterson took a chance on her. But she had to take the necessary steps to get there.

Slowly, over the days and months, her quilt, along with the stories bringing the next issue of *Quilter's Heart* to fruition, had become more than a job to her. She'd stitched her heart and soul into every seam of the quilt. The challenge with Ben, along with working on her project, was in God's hands. She'd put her faith to the test and see where it led her.

Molly tried to control her nerves as Paul drove their dad's truck through the Hillsborough River State Park. They pulled into parking lot #4, where she'd meet her team at the kayak launch.

Today, she had two things to worry about. How different would it be kayaking the river when she'd gotten used to the lake? And would the kids accept her or make the adventure more complicated than necessary?

"Are you ready?" Paul asked, as he yanked the truck gate down.

Molly blew out a gusty breath. "As I'll ever be."

She helped Paul tug the borrowed kayak from the truck bed. Together they hauled it to the water's edge.

"How's your shoulder?" she asked, trying to carry most of the weight.

He'd removed the sling but judging by the way he grimaced and favored his shoulder by keeping his arm close to his side, it still bothered him. "Better. It'll take some time to heal. I'm not very patient."

She snorted.

"Mom's been after me to sit around and rest. Did she forget I don't like inactivity? She's always fussing and worrying."

Molly grinned. "Welcome to my world."

"I never noticed it when we were growing up."

"Because you were never home."

"Yeah." He sent her a guilty look. "I'm sorry. I should have hung around more."

She tried to keep her tone light, as if the conversation didn't hit a nerve. "Staying at home wouldn't have changed anything."

Paul didn't miss it a beat. "No, but now I get why you don't visit Mom and Dad. It's more than just the fussing and you know it."

Yeah, she did. "At least Dad didn't get all weird when I told him about the challenge. Unlike Mom."

"Read you the riot act, huh?"

"You could say so. I'm surprised she hasn't called me every day with a list of reasons why I should stay away from the water."

Paul chuckled. "She'd be impressed if she could see you. Hey, I'm impressed. You've gotten the hang of kayaking in no time."

Molly basked in her brother's praise. "Amazingly enough, I find being on the water soothing, provided the water is calm. I can think, you know, clear out the stress of the day and enjoy being in the moment." She gazed over the gently flowing river. Majestic cypress trees rose from the shallow riverbank. Dense green foliage lined the woods. Spanish moss draped tree limbs. Birds cried out over the sound of conversation between adults and excited kids.

"I've also enjoyed pushing myself at something new. For so many years I'd convinced myself I couldn't tackle any outdoor activities. I was afraid I might get sick. Just the opposite has happened. The physical activity is making me feel . . . healthy."

"Better than quilting?"

"No, never. Just different." She busied herself by pulling her equipment from the bag Jed sent with them. "You'll laugh when I tell you I came up with a quilt design the last time I went out on the lake. When I got home, I sketched out the basic idea. It's going to be different shades of blue with a pattern of movement."

"Here your boss thought you'd have a tough time with the challenge, and you've ended up with another feature for your magazine."

"Funny how these things work out." She glanced over at the adults gathered some feet away. "I suppose I should go over and introduce myself. Find out what's in store for me."

"I'll finish getting things ready here."

She started to walk away. Paul stopped her by laying a hand on her shoulder. "I'm glad you called me. We've missed out on a lot together."

"Yes, we have." She noted his pensive expression, telling her he had more to say.

"In the military we get close, especially with the guys you work and live with on a daily basis. I've seen things I wish I hadn't. Been in places I wish I didn't have to be. The Corps becomes a family." He paused. "Almost made me forget I have my own family right here at home."

Molly smiled, her heart squeezing tight with joy. She hugged him. "Love you, too," she whispered in his ear.

He cleared his throat and held her at arm's length. "Now go. Be outdoorsy."

Right. Her brother had faith in her. She'd do him proud.

She joined the adults to find out more about the group, Parents Fight Back. Founded by parents whose children had gotten into trouble at school or with law enforcement, each month the parents got together to support some type of outing, whether it be community service, physical activity, or just fun.

They'd decided to make the kayaking excursion a way for the kids to get exercise and also as a way to raise money, much like a 5k walk or run with each participant soliciting pledges. Today the group gathered for a trial run. Next week, the official event would satisfy Molly's part of the challenge. How Charlie found out about the group Molly didn't know, but she had to hand it to him, it was right up her alley. Well, the fund-raising part, not the actual kayaking.

Since Molly tended to be drawn to community organizations, in the back of her mind she tucked the idea of featuring this group in Mr. Masterson's new magazine. Just the sort of story the magazine would feature.

The leader explained the day's events. From the put-in point, the paddlers would travel three miles one way down the river to end up at Dead River Park. A perfect place for beginners, the first stretch of the river, while very scenic, had no strong currents. Those not kayaking would drive the vehicles to the next access point and rendezvous with the paddlers there.

Thankfully, she'd become comfortable every time she went out in the kayak. And surprise, surprise, she didn't ache after being on the water. She chuckled to herself at the thought of her arms having gained some muscle definition she'd never had before. And she'd dropped a few pounds. Now she understood why people liked exercise.

Her group consisted of two lanky teen boys with shaggy hair falling over their eyes, coupled with a mile-long attitude streak. The lone girl, about sixteen, stood off to the side as the groups gathered together, waiting for instructions. Molly covertly watched her. The girl stared at the ground. Shy or standoffish, Molly couldn't tell, but knew enough to know if they didn't work together, the boys in their group would be more than glad to make them miserable.

She walked to the girl, pasting a confident smile on her lips. "Hi, I'm Molly. What's your name?"

"Sabrina."

"Cool name."

The girl shrugged and kept her gaze downcast.

"Have you been kayaking before?"

"Couple times."

"Looking forward to today?"

Sabrina shrugged again.

Okay. A tough nut to crack. Molly had developed the art of drawing people out of their shells after talking to plenty of women while volunteering at Second Chances. She could wait for Sabrina to get comfortable. "I'm not much of an outdoors person myself, but learning how to kayak is kind of job-related."

"So you don't have a choice about being here, either?"

"Well, I have a choice. I wasn't too happy at first, but being on the water has been kind of fun. I'm pushing myself, you know what I mean?"

Sabrina met Molly's gaze for the first time. Behind those hazel eyes and sulky attitude stood a girl not sure of her surroundings or how to handle herself. Molly could relate.

"My brother and coworkers are afraid I can't finish." Molly nodded toward the boys. "Same attitude from those guys?"

"Yeah. Mark and Jason. The reason we're in the same group is because our parents know each other."

"You don't like them?"

She scuffed her sneaker in the dirt. "They're okay, I guess. Mark can be nice."

Molly hid a grin. Sabrina's reaction made her think of Ben. She hoped she didn't get the same goofy smile when she was around him. If he, or anyone in the office, found out about her attraction to him, she'd never live it down.

"I have to say, I've never been very cool around guys. My one big crush in high school ended in disaster. And I don't have a boyfriend right now."

Sabrina looked over at the boys. "Mark is fun when he's not with Jason. But they always hang out together."

Hmm. Could Molly do anything to help Sabrina? She thought about it for a few moments, running different scenarios through her mind. Then it hit her.

"I have an idea."

Sabrina cast her a glance saying, I doubt it. She'd come up with enough impromptu ideas at Second Chances to know Sabrina required a fresh outlook on the situation.

"I have a feeling the boys have counted us out. Let's stick together. Show them they can't intimidate us."

Sabrina's face brightened, but still she held back. "They think they're good at everything."

"Nobody is good at everything, so I say we prove them wrong. Girl power." She held up her hand to high five and Sabrina responded by slapping her palm.

"Do you think your idea will work?" Sabrina asked.

"We won't know unless we give it a try." Molly glimpsed determination in Sabrina's eyes. "C'mon over and meet my brother."

Molly led the way and introduced the two. "Sabrina and I want to show up the boys. Any pointers?"

"Don't show any fear. They'll eat you up otherwise."

"Nice visual."

He shrugged. "It's what guys do."

Molly threw an arm over Sabrina's thin shoulders. "Ready?" she asked.

Sabrina nodded, excitement clear on her face. "Ready."

While Sabrina bent over to pick up a paddle, Molly mouthed "Thank you" to Paul. He smiled and strode to the truck to travel the four miles to the next access point.

Mark and Jason, punching and kicking at each other, joined Molly and Sabrina.

"Hey, guys." Molly ramped up her cheery voice. "Looking forward to being in your group."

Jason shrugged and laughed, "You're never going to keep up with us."

Mark stopped beside Molly and shyly glanced at Sabrina. "What's up?"

"Nothing," Sabrina answered.

Molly rolled her eyes. These two had a long way to go if they ever wanted a relationship.

Which for some reason made her wonder about Ben's love life. Or if he had one. And if he did? None of her business. Ugh. She was as bad as Sabrina.

Before long, everyone had their kayaks in the water and started to paddle downriver. As expected, the boys took off while Molly and Sabrina hung back, getting used to the environment and enjoying the lush scenery.

"Have you been involved with these folks long?" Molly asked, encouraging conversation between them.

"A little while. My parents thought hanging with these kids would be a good idea."

"They don't like your friends?"

Sabrina shot her a sharp look.

"Just asking. Not judging."

They paddled for a while before Sabrina said, "I got into some trouble. Some girls I started hanging out with lifted make-up from a store. They got caught, but I got a warning because I didn't have anything on me."

"Because you didn't take anything?"

"I didn't even know what they had planned."

"Wrong place, wrong time."

Sabrina sent her a cautious look. "Yeah."

"Do you know what kind of friends they are?"

"Not very good ones. They dropped me after we all got in trouble."

"I guess you learned the hard way what kind of people to steer clear of."

"Whatever."

Molly laughed. Teen angst. She didn't miss it one teeny, tiny bit. "When you find the right people, it's great. I have a group of women I've hung around with since I was sixteen."

"That's a long time."

"It is. But worth it. I trust them and they never let me down."

The kayakers in front of Molly and Sabrina widened the gap between them but Molly didn't care. Sunlight dappled through the trees limbs, casting shadows over the water. Wet earth mingled with the dank scent of decaying foliage. With no current to contend with, they paddled with ease. Birds chirped overhead and an occasional insect zipped by. Molly had worried about transitioning from a lake to the river, but so far so good.

"So what do you like to do?" Molly asked.

Sabrina paddled like a pro. "I like books. Movies."

"Me, too. Have you ever quilted?"

"No."

"I was your age when I started. You know those girls who didn't fit in anywhere? I was one of them. When the ladies asked me to join them, I thought why not?" She paused for a moment. "If you're interested, I'd be happy to teach you."

"I don't know."

"If you decide you want to, the invitation is always open," Molly assured her.

Up ahead, the boys slowed down as they steered the kayaks close to the bank. Something on shore must have caught their attention because they pointed into the foliage.

"Now would be a good time to show them what we've got," Molly said.

As one, they paddled to the same rhythm, speeding up to pass the boys. Once by, Molly heard one of them yell. She glanced at Sabrina, nodding as a signal to pick up the pace.

Time passed quickly and before Molly knew it, they'd reached the take-out point. Some of the kids still sat in their kayaks, talking and goofing around.

Sabrina grinned. "We beat them."

"Indeed we did." Molly grinned back at her new partner. "Up for some fun?"

"Like what?"

Aiming at the boys, Molly mimicked shoveling her paddle through the water. Sabrina, catching on, smiled and nodded.

As they boys glided to them, Sabrina waited for Mark to come up beside her, then shoved a paddle of water at him. He sputtered and wiped his face. His eyes narrowed and he returned the favor. Not to be left out, Jason splashed Molly. The cold water hit her in the face, shocking her system. She licked her lips, tasting the coppery tang of the water as it trickled down her cheeks. Lifting her paddle over her head, she belted out a battle cry and returned Jason's splashes with a vengeance. The remaining kids circling around them joined in, laughing and yelling, engaged in a full-scale water war.

Once the antics wore down, Molly paddled to Sabrina. "Guess we showed them."

Sabrina laughed, her hair soaked to her head, her eyes filled with merriment. "Awesome."

"See, some adults can be fun to hang out with."

"Thanks, Molly. I had a blast. Can't wait until next week."

"With you and I together as a team, we'll knock their socks, er, paddles off."

Sabrina giggled. "Promise me next time we'll have as much fun."

"Promise." Molly paddled to the bank where Paul waited to help her out.

"I always knew you'd make a worthy opponent," he told her.

"I learned it from the best."

Easing her way out of the kayak, Molly waded in the shin-high water, guiding the boat to Paul. He grabbed hold of one end while she pushed the other. When he had it partially out of the river, Molly dug her toes in the mud to climb the slippery bank. As she did, her sneakers slipped and she tottered. She went still, trying to balance her stance, but her feet slid toward the water. The momentum had her swinging her arms in the air as she tried to keep upright. Failing, she stretched her arms out in front of her as she fell, landing with all her weight on her right arm. Pain slammed into her wrist and radiated up her arm. Her breath caught in her throat. She knelt in the water, cradling her wrist against her chest, trying not to cry.

Paul jumped in beside her in a flash. "Are you okay?" he asked as he took hold of her good arm and helped her to dry land.

Blinking back tears, she took a deep breath. "It hurts, but I'll be okay."

"Don't be a hero, Sis."

Right. If anything, she'd reverted back to the kid who had to be protected. Hating the idea, she straightened her shoulders, shaking off her latest disaster.

Paul took hold of her aching hand and gently probed her wrist. She winced.

"I can't tell if it's sprained. We should go to the clinic just to be sure."

"Give me a few minutes." She refused to be babied. "Maybe it will stop throbbing."

"What kind of a coach would I be if we didn't get your injury diagnosed?"

She rolled her eyes, but agreed as the pain worsened. "Please don't tell Mom and Dad. Promise to keep this between us."

His dark eyes narrowed. "If you let me take you to a clinic."

"Okay."

Paul made quick time loading the truck, making Molly feel guilty. He had his own injury to nurse back to health. By the time they got on the road, her wrist throbbed and grew even puffier.

What would Mr. Masterson think when he found out? Or Ben? Any setback gave him a definite advantage. More importantly, would her injury keep her from finishing the quilt? It couldn't. She didn't have the time. Pursing her lips together, she stared out the window, the thought of losing the competition settling on her shoulders.

10

Ben stood outside Nora's front door Sunday afternoon, the spicy aroma of fried chicken wafting from the bucket in his hand. He'd been invited to the once-a-month potluck lunch Nora held with the women from the quilting group and their families. He'd tried to beg off, but Nora wouldn't hear of it. She'd even gotten him to commit to attending church. He'd made the service, his first real attempt in years. It had felt odd, being around so many believers. But it had brought peace, too.

While he'd been reluctant to attend many professional functions, he'd always stayed clear of more personal get-togethers. The same questions haunted him. Would he fit in here? Would he have anything in common with these folks? The whole point of accepting the invitation was to get him involved with people on a personal level.

Never a quitter, he didn't plan to become one now. He pressed the doorbell and heard a loud yell. "It's open."

Squaring his shoulders, he entered and made his way to the crowded kitchen, where women scurried around. Nora waved at him.

"Find an empty space for the bucket. We'll take care of it from here."

He cleared a space on the counter and stood, waiting to be told what to do next.

"Go out back and visit," Nora instructed.

Straightening his shoulders, Ben ventured to the backyard to meet husbands and children. The contained chaos should be second nature to him after all the years spent traveling with a crew. For a guy used to being in the thick of things, he didn't know what to do here. One of the men engaged him in conversation. Before long Nora and the ladies came outside and they all prayed a blessing over the food. Ben filled his plate from the buffet and took a seat under a tree, away from the crowd. After a few minutes Nora joined him.

"A little overwhelming?"

The woman did know how to get to the crux of the matter. "Some." He faced her with an arched brow. "You had everything planned out, didn't you?"

"Why do you think I asked you to come? It time for you to make some friends."

"Thanks. I appreciate it."

They ate for a few moments in silence, until Ben had to ask the question nagging at him since he'd arrived. "So is Molly coming?"

Nora grinned. "She'll be here. She had something to do with her brother."

"I know she went kayaking yesterday." It had driven him crazy, knowing where she was, but giving her space to figure out her part in the challenge. Twice he found himself pocketing his keys, ready to jump in his SUV to check her progress. He had to keep his space, otherwise he'd come off like a presumptuous pain in her neck.

"I haven't spoken to her in a few days." Nora chuckled. "Molly in a kayak. How is her training coming?"

"I don't know. I've decided to stay away. Let her deal with the challenge on her own."

Nora rested her plate on her lap. "Have you thought about what will happen when the challenge is over?"

"One of us will get the job." He noticed Nora's dubious look. "But it's not what you're asking."

"Smart man." She patted his arm. "How will you feel if Molly wins?"

"I haven't considered the possibility."

"You're much too cocky, young man. She may surprise you."

She already had, but not in the ways Nora thought. When they were apart, Molly invaded his thoughts. When they were together, he enjoyed her company more than any woman he'd ever met. And evidenced by the way his chest swelled whenever she came into his orbit, he suspected he'd passed the like stage some weeks ago.

"Then how will you feel if she loses?" Nora asked, pulling him from his thoughts.

"I don't want to think about it." The mental image of her crestfallen face had appeared in his dreams on numerous occasions. For that reason alone, he dreaded the outcome. "Molly's a lot more together than she gives herself credit for."

"You've noticed, hmm."

"She'd be good at the job, but so would I."

"Have you taken time to pray about it?"

"I did this morning. I have to admit, I'm kinda rusty."

"It will all work out, I have no doubt."

"I hope. I don't want Molly to get hurt by this challenge."

"Then make sure she doesn't."

They went back to eating when a loud commotion sounded in the kitchen. Molly, followed by her brother, walked into the backyard.

"Sorry we're late."

She stood in the bright afternoon sun, her hair pulled back, wearing another feminine dress. Her gold earrings glinted in the bright sunlight. He couldn't take his eyes from her. His gaze took her all in, from her jeweled sandals, to the large beach bag she carried, to the bandage wrapped around her wrist. Wait. Bandage?

He jumped up and stormed toward her. "What happened?"

"I slipped and fell at the river yesterday. It's not a big deal."

She didn't miss the disgruntled look he exchanged with her brother. "Why didn't you watch out for her?"

"I did watch out. I couldn't keep her from slipping in the mud."

He glared at Paul before turning back to Molly. "This is it. This challenge is over."

"Whoa. Who made you king of the challenge?"

"Molly—"

"Ben, don't worry. It's not even a sprain. My wrist only hurts a little today. Besides, I could trip and fall on my way into the office."

"I still don't like it."

She touched his arm. "I appreciate the concern, but I'll be fine."

Ben took a step back and breathed. Okay, he'd panicked when he saw the bandage, but he needed to calm down here. It wasn't like she'd injured herself so badly she'd ended up in the hospital.

So why did he feel like he'd been kicked in the gut?

Because Molly stood there with her wrist taped up and shadows under her eyes. And you weren't there to protect her.

Having been involved in so many outdoor activities, he knew it wasn't unusual for someone to get a minor sprain or cut. He'd nursed a few bruises himself over the years. But this was Molly, who looked better than ever since the challenge started. A healthy glow brightened her skin and daily she grew more confident about herself and her surroundings.

It had been so long since he cared about a woman, his gut reaction to her injury surprised him. He may want the promotion, but not at the expense of her safety. Getting hurt crossed the line. No way could her injury go unnoticed.

As if reading his mind, Molly grabbed hold of Ben's arm with her good hand and dragged him around the side of the house.

"I told you, it's not a problem."

"It already is a problem."

"Promise me you won't say anything."

"I can't."

"Please." Her blues eyes pleaded with him. "I don't want to be taken out of the running because of a clumsy incident on my part. If you say anything, Mr. Masterson will end the challenge. He'll think I can't handle pressure."

"Like you said at the beginning, he should base the promotion on who is best for the job."

"But he isn't. And I don't want to lose out because I had an accident." She removed her hand from his arm. "I had a good time yesterday. Please don't ruin what I've started by tattling on me."

He arched one brow. "Tattle?"

"It's not a very manly thing to do. And we both know you're a manly man."

Her teasing, husky voice, shot straight to his heart. He couldn't refuse her request, even though it went against his protective instincts. From the first day in Masterson's office when he'd issued the challenge, Ben never considered he'd act on those instincts. Never thought he'd care enough about Molly to want to keep her from harm.

As clear as day, he realized what he'd once felt for Cassie had been eclipsed by his feelings for Molly. He thought Cassie had been the one person with the power to make him feel deeply. Wrong. When had Molly, the intelligent, brave woman who stood before him, burrowed into his mind and heart? The one woman who had as much to lose as he did?

She squinted up at him, waiting for his decision.

Right then and there, he realized she'd cracked the wall around his heart. "I'll let you slide this once. Any more injuries and we're done."

She released a puff of air. "Thank you."

"But you have to promise me you'll be more careful."

"I will. And it was a freak thing. We'd been splashing in the water and I guess I didn't realize how slippery the bank would be."

"Just to be sure, I'm coming the next time you go out in the kayak."

She frowned. "No need. I have Paul."

"Well, now you have me, too."

"Ben—"

"No arguments or I go to Masterson."

"Fine." She crossed her arms over her chest.

The pressure in his chest eased at her pique. "Go ahead."

Her brows angled in confusion. "What?"

"Go ahead and stomp your foot. You know you want to."

"Yeah. Right on top of your size tens."

They stood there a few more moments before Molly's eyes met his. Their gazes locked and he couldn't, no, didn't dare move. She blinked, her eyes so blue and luminous behind her contacts. He couldn't stop himself from reaching out to run a finger over her soft cheek. She tilted her head into his caress. Reading the movement as a positive sign, Ben lowered his head with every intention of kissing her.

Until a bunch of kids rounded the corner of the house chasing after a soccer ball. Jolted out of the moment, Molly jumped back, her hand covering her cheek where he'd touched her.

"Um, I need to see Nora," she said, backing away from him.

"Right. I should go mingle."

Mingle? What was he thinking? Had he lost his mind when he decided to kiss Molly? Not only had he made things awkward between them, he now had to honor his word and talk to the other guests.

All because of a woman who had him thinking with his heart, not as his rival.

Ben kept a safe distance from Molly, still disconcerted over their near kiss, yet wishing he'd carried through. He ran a hand through his hair. She drove him crazy on so many levels, least of which would be the outcome of the challenge. And how they'd react toward each other after one of them lost the challenge.

By late afternoon, Ben had had enough conversation for the day. He'd made an effort to speak to every person present, including the children. So far so good, until Paul cornered him.

"So, you think you have my sister beat?"

"Look, it's nothing personal." Right. And if he said it enough times he might believe it.

"She's serious about winning, otherwise she'd never put herself in a situation to get hurt."

"I don't like seeing your sister hurt, either. For any reason. I tried to talk her out of continuing the challenge, but she refused."

A glimmer of a smile touched Paul's lips. "Getting a promotion means a lot to her. My sister has never been one to move too far out of her comfort zone or get involved in any type of outdoor activity. She's working overtime to prove herself."

"I get it, you're looking out for her."

"I don't want her disappointed in any way." Paul crossed his arms over his chest as he viewed Ben. "Catch my drift?"

Great. Had her brother noticed the attraction between them? Ben didn't know how to respond because he was still trying to sort out their attraction himself.

"I have no intention of hurting your sister," he told the scowling man standing in front of him. "You can trust me."

"I don't know you well enough to trust you," Paul countered. "So I guess I'm going to have to take your word. Be forewarned. I'm going to keep an eye on you."

Brotherly concern wrapped in bravado. He may not have a family, but he understood the sentiment behind Paul's words.

"What are you two up to?" Molly asked as she joined them, a frown marring her brow. "You aren't causing any trouble, are you Paul?"

"Just making sure Ben knows where I stand."

Molly rolled her eyes. "Ignore him, Ben."

Ben hadn't gotten where he had in life to ignore an unspoken threat when he heard one. And since family dynamics could be tricky, he had no intention of taking Paul's advice lightly.

"C'mon, Sis. I need to get home."

"Um . . . I need to go over to the center."

He frowned. "You didn't mention going to Second Chances earlier."

"Because I knew you'd give me a hard time."

"With your wrist taped up, you should head home."

She rolled her eyes. "For the tenth time, I'm fine. And I promised."

"What's so important you have to go there on a Sunday afternoon?"

"It's not a big deal. I just have something to take care of."

"I have somewhere to be, but I can drop you off. You can call me when you need to go back home."

"I can take her," Ben offered, before he'd thought it through.

Paul measured him up. "You sure?"

"I don't have any plans."

Paul glanced at his sister. "Okay with you?"

Molly bit her lip and cast a glance at Ben. "I can always ask Nora for a ride, if it's too much trouble."

"Why bother her? Besides, she probably wants to rest after a long day with company. And we'll get some time to talk." About what he didn't know. A lecture on safety might be a good start.

"I guess."

Could she sound any less excited?

Paul leaned over to give his sister a quick hug. "I'll call you."

And then Paul blew out the door, leaving Ben with a sassy blonde who shifted his heart into overdrive. "Ready to go?"

"Sure. Thanks, Ben."

He shrugged. "Think of it as me giving a helping hand."

She brightened up, a sly smile tugging her lips. "I'm glad you think so."

He groaned. "Why do I get the feeling I just agreed to some unknown project of yours."

"Because you did."

They said their good-byes, and soon Ben had her settled on the passenger side of his SUV. He kept trying to convince himself his actions had to do with community involvement and making friends, but when he got a whiff of Molly's sweet perfume as he climbed behind the wheel, he knew otherwise.

Molly kept her fidgeting to a minimum as Ben backed out of the driveway. As many times as she'd dropped whatever she was doing to help in one emergency or another, she'd never had a tagalong before. Now she did. A tall, handsome, tagalong.

Sneaking a peek at her driver, she muffled the sigh promising to escape her lips. She admired his strong profile. The steady hands on the wheel. And couldn't ignore the excitement bubbling in her. The fact he'd volunteered to spend time with her, even though he had no idea what he'd volunteered for beyond being her chauffeur, filled her with joy.

It seems she and Ben were destined to be thrown together, even when not work-related. She wasn't complaining. The more she'd came to know Ben, the more she saw a side of him she realized he hid around most people.

How many meetings or work-related events had they attended when Ben shone in the spotlight? Too many to count, but each of those times he spoke about the job or his exploits. Never about Ben the man. His confidence had been the first thing she noticed about him, but today, at Nora's, she noticed he held himself back. Not when he'd made his displeasure with her clear, but when he'd interacted with her friends. It was almost as if he had to make himself sit down and talk. Or ask questions. She could have sworn she saw panic in his eyes when one of Nora's grandsons asked him to toss a baseball with him. The man lived and breathed sports, so why would throwing a ball around bother him?

She took it upon herself to eavesdrop. Not the entire time, in fear he'd figure her out, but whenever she passed by. And in every conversation he always deflected the topic from him or his past. Why? Did he have something to hide? And if he did, did she want to know about it?

Who was she kidding? Of course she did. Otherwise, she wouldn't have let him drive her to the center for some quality time.

"So you got called to the center again?" he asked once they started traveling the main road.

She twisted in her seat to face him. "I have a confession to make."

He glanced at her. "Doesn't sound good."

She laughed. "When I told Paul about the picnic, he insisted on driving me over, like I'm some sort of invalid. I couldn't say no. But I also couldn't tell him why I need to go to the center."

"Are you going to keep me in suspense?"

"The contractor finished the drywall and it needs to be painted before we can begin to move back into the old location. I promised to do the work."

"On Sunday?"

"The director failed to line up a volunteer crew to do the job, and the contractor needs everything finished up for the final inspection."

"So you're going to do it all alone?"

"Well, since you offered, I kind of hoped I could sweet talk you into slapping some paint on the walls. You can master a brush, can't you?"

"Not very subtle and yes, I've painted a time or two."

"Great. With the two of us working together, we'll knock it out in no time."

"The director of the center is not very good at her job." He tossed her a pointed look again. "So why does everything seem to fall back to you?"

"Believe me, I've asked myself the same question plenty of times. I always make time when they need me so I'm sort of the go-to person since she's come aboard."

"Can't you complain to someone?"

"The board of directors, I suppose, but it hasn't come to that yet."

"I've been with you three times now when you've covered for her. Seems like a problem to me."

"I have faith it will all work out."

"Faith in you or God?"

"God, of course."

He shook his head. "Have you ever heard of burning candles at both ends?"

"What can I say? I spent so many years cooped up at home. I guess I'm making up for it now."

"Care to explain?"

"I had lots of allergies when I was a kid. Because of my bouts of sickness, my parents kept me indoors. Overprotective is their middle name."

"Aren't most parents?"

"Not to this extreme." She waved her hand. "Anyway, I'm not troubled so much now, so I can get outside, do more."

"Like kayaking?"

"It's kind of growing on me."

"Doesn't sound good for me."

She smiled. Finally. He took her as a threat for the promotion.

They pulled up to the building. Ben parked the car while Molly removed the keys from her purse. She unlocked the door and they entered the empty building to find paint buckets and brushes piled in one corner.

"So, boss, where do you want to start?"

"Depends. Do you like to roll or cut in?"

He nodded to her wrist. "In light of your injury, why don't you roll while I cut in."

"I'm not out of commission. Sheesh." She held up her beach bag. "Let me change into work clothes. I'm sorry I don't have anything for you."

"While you change, I'll run out to the dollar store down the street, buy some work clothes and be right back."

Could her day get any better? She had Ben to herself for a few hours. She changed, folding her dress and accessories into the bag. She pulled her hair into a ponytail before exiting the bathroom, just as Ben walked back through the door.

"You were fast."

"Not many customers lined up on a Sunday afternoon."

"While you get changed, I'm going to start outlining the windows." She retrieved blue painter's tape from a plastic bag and went to work.

Ben returned, decked out in cargo shorts and T-shirt. He opened a bucket, poured the creamy yellow paint into a pan, and slid the round brush on the end of the extended pole for Molly's use.

She had two more windows to tape around before painting. "I can't believe how new drywall makes such a big difference. After the fire we couldn't get rid of the acrid smell. The walls were streaked with a coating of black ash."

"Yeah. You'd never know there was a fire."

They got busy, engrossed for a few minutes before Molly broke the silence. "So, care to tell me why the promotion is so important to you?"

"Everyone wants to be rewarded for their work," he said as he found a smaller pan to pour paint into and climbed up the stepladder to begin edging.

"You've been here a short while. And you've done tons of things to be rewarded for your work. You've even been on television. After all your global traipsing around, why end up here? Seems to me it might be more personal."

She noticed he stopped painting for a moment. Had she hit the mark?

"When I took the job, Masterson agreed to keep me in one place. Traveling gets old after a while."

"Okay. I could see staying put as a decisive reason. Anything else?"

"Has anyone ever mentioned you're nosy?"

"It's the journalist in me." She cut the tape off and moved to the next window. "Besides, I've had experience getting people to open up to me. How do you think I get the girls at the center to talk?"

"Makes sense."

"And you're changing the subject again."

"I don't want to talk about me," he countered.

"Fine. Just give me one tidbit about yourself and I'll leave you alone."

"You're relentless."

"Not a tidbit, but I'll take it as a compliment."

He went silent for a long time. Molly figured he was biding his time, hoping she'd lay off. Poor, deluded man if he thought otherwise.

"I have a new condo without any furniture," he said so fast the words ran together.

"What?" She frowned over the unexpected words.

He set his brush in the nearby pan. "I've traveled so many years I didn't have a home base. Now I do, but I'm starting from scratch."

"Wow. Okay." She hid a grin as she finished the window and went to pick up the pole to roll the paint on the wall. "Need some help picking out a couch?"

"Funny." He continued edging. "The point is, I'm starting a new chapter of my life."

"And it should be an exciting time." She peeked at his serious expression again. "You're really alone? I know about your parents, but no friends? Girlfriend?"

"I do have some buddies from high school who I've been reconnecting with. And believe me, traveling isn't good for dating. I've come back here to start over. I want to create new friendships, new experiences with people I hope will become an important part of my life."

"Tall order."

"Especially since I've been gone for a long time."

She got her wish, Ben talking about himself. But she still needed him to clarify one important point. "So I'm guessing no girlfriend?"

"No. No girlfriend."

Sweet relief coursed through her. His admission didn't constitute a move on her, but the fact he had no significant other gave her hope. This charismatic man had regular, everyday issues like most people. Good to know.

"So the bottom line is?"

"We both have our reasons for wanting the promotion," he said.

"About that, thanks for treating me as a viable opponent. You don't know how much it means to me."

"You're tough. I can't imagine you not going all in."

She thought about his statement for a moment. "To be honest, it's new territory for me. I always shy away from conflict."

"C'mon, you're a natural."

"Hardly. Remember I told you my parents are overprotective? Well, their behavior set me up to believe I shouldn't go after anything if it might hurt me."

"And kayaking would fall in that category."

"Exactly."

"Explains why your brother was so wigged out over your wrist. I don't blame him. You shouldn't have been asked to do anything if it could cause an injury."

"Like I told Paul, I could have tripped and fallen anywhere." She held up her taped wrist. "It just so happened to be on a slippery river bank."

"Still—"

"Still, nothing. I wanted to be there. I enjoyed my time on the river."

"So what, you're finally being rebellious?"

She considered his statement. "I never looked at it like that."

"Okay, maybe not rebellious, but more decisive."

"True."

"I imagine your parents aren't thrilled with your part in the challenge."

"Nope. But I stood up to them and told them I was participating whether they liked it or not."

Ben climbed down the ladder for more paint. "I don't mean to rain on your parade, but you're fortunate you have your family."

She almost argued the point until she remembered Ben's history. "Sorry. I don't mean to sound ungrateful. It's just . . . as a family . . . we've grown apart over the years."

"Too bad. There are a lot of people who'd give anything to have what you have."

She'd spent so many years angry with her folks, she'd never considered what life might be like without them. "I guess for so long I felt like a burden to my parents. I always wondered if they loved me."

Ben climbed back up the ladder. "I'm sure it's tough being a parent. How much leeway do you give your kids and still protect them? I know my folks were always there for me. Maybe because I was an only child. But as I got older, we just liked hanging around together." He paused for a moment, his voice rough when he said, "It was tough when they died."

"I'm so sorry, Ben."

Seeing how his loss had affected him made Molly realize she still had a chance with her parents if she wanted to try and change things. Could she? The question bothered her. Ben had a different outlook on family than she did. For the first time in a long time, she stopped to examine her family relationship, wondering if they could come together as a whole, healthy unit.

"Is the way you grew up why you're so quick to help the women at the center?" Ben asked, getting right to the heart of the matter. "Because of your relationship with your parents? You feel a connection with them?"

She'd never thought in those terms, but what he said made sense. "Not consciously, but I know how the heart aches when you don't feel loved." And to think, she had her family to thank for her volunteer work, as Ben pointed out.

"Yeah. Another thing I miss with my parents being gone."

How could she respond? Except maybe to view her family with a little more thanks.

They worked in companionable silence for a while before a thought occurred to her. "Can I ask you something?"

"Again?" he deadpanned.

"Yeah, again." She dipped the roller in the pan to add more paint to the roller. "Does it bother you to be around the quilting group? They're pretty close and tend to be just as nosy as me."

"Yeah, I noticed. Figured they got the go-ahead to ask questions from you."

"Sorry, but no. It's their normal operating procedure."

He grinned. "Nora and I have had a few in-depth conversations."

"If they were getting into my business, I would have asked them to stop."

"Molly, it's been a long time since anyone took an interest in my personal life. I don't let very many people in, but Nora and the others haven't crossed any lines. We've made our own connection of sorts."

She nodded, working the roller in a smooth motion. "And I suppose you're tough enough to handle them?"

"I'm not sure, but I know I like them."

Molly should have felt bad for intruding on Ben's personal life, but she didn't. He needed people in his life, people who cared. Nora and the other ladies filled the void.

Connection. The word Ben used. She liked it. So much of what she wanted to accomplish by bringing the Hearts Entwined quilt to the public focused on connection. From Molly coming up with the initial idea, to the women who sent the fabric, to the readers of *Quilter's Heart,* and the people at the Expo who would bid to take home her creation. Connections.

"I shouldn't care," she said, "since the harder they are on you, the better for me."

"Trust me, quilting hasn't been a walk in the park. We still haven't finished the one we're working on."

"Didn't turn out as easy as you thought?"

"No. I admire your patience for all the fancy needlework."

"Most people don't fathom the hours spent making a quality quilt. It's an art form to me."

"Just like sports is a way of life for me."

"Which I'll never understand."

He chuckled.

It took them close to ninety minutes, but they had the walls completed before the sun went down. While Ben closed up the bucket, Molly removed the tape she'd put up earlier. They carried the brush and roller out back to rinse off under the outside spigot.

"Thanks, Ben. I appreciate your help."

He shrugged. "I didn't have anything going on."

"Still, you lost your entire Sunday afternoon."

"I enjoyed working. Feels good to be connected to something important."

She beamed at him. "My feelings exactly."

"Now I understand why you volunteer."

"And I can count on you from now on?"

"Just ask."

"Cool. Oh, and please don't rat me out to my brother. He won't be happy knowing we came here to work."

"Your secret is safe with me."

He shook out his brush, while Molly placed the rolling brush up against the building to dry. He turned his head and met her gaze. "Guess we both learned a thing or two about each other today. We make a pretty good team."

Yes, they did. She turned off the water to stare into his eyes. Her heart raced. Why now, after spending the entire afternoon together, did her hormones have to go haywire?

Because there is more to him than meets the eye and you can't help falling for him. Because he's so close you can feel his body heat. Because you want to be more than just a good team.

She closed her eyes for a half-second and caught her breath.

"Molly? Are you okay?"

Nope. Not since the day Ben sauntered into Master's Publishing, his handsome face smiling at her, his confidence a mile high. She hadn't been the same since. She opened her eyes. "Sorry. I just . . ."

His gaze lowered to her lips. Would he kiss her? Oh, she wanted him to. More than anything. But where could a relationship go for them? One would get the cushy upstairs office and the other would be the loser. Not a very even playing field if you asked her.

His warm hand wrapped around hers. Heat zinged up her arm and straight to her heart. He must have sensed his effect on her because he slowly, deliberately lowered his head and brushed his lips over hers.

She would have gasped if she'd been able, but her mind went blank. The man of her dreams, kissing her. She leaned closer. The kiss went deeper. Giddy and in awe at the same time, Molly returned his kiss. Because this was Ben, the man she couldn't get out of her heart.

Much too soon, he broke the kiss. She stared up at him, still caught up in the moment. A car horn blared in the distance.

Reality slapped her. What was she thinking? Kissing her rival? She took a step back and cleared her throat. "We should head home. We have a long week ahead of us."

He frowned, but released his hold.

"Let's go lock up."

They finished in strained silence and before long were back in Ben's SUV headed home. She'd learned more about Ben in a few short hours today than in the previous months working with him. Now she'd take the information and tuck it away in her heart, because there was no way she could act on her feelings towards him.

The fact they were rivals sealed the deal. Yes, he may have sent her heated looks today. Yes, he'd thrilled her with the most awesome kiss she'd ever experienced. But the kiss didn't change the fact he never came right out and told her his true feelings. For all she knew, he considered her anywhere from a mild attraction to a troublesome coworker. No way would she put herself out there, embarrass herself by inquiring, and have him crush her with an answer she might not like.

"Thanks for the lift," she said as he parked in front of her apartment building. The mood in the vehicle had become somber. "And sorry for prying," she teased.

He chuckled. "You're kind of growing on me."

"You say so now," she said as she slipped out of the SUV. "Wait till next week. You may change your mind."

"Doubt it'll happen."

She stood bathed in the light of the street lamp, hoping beyond hope his words were true.

11

Monday morning, Molly arrived to work before her coworkers. She spread the quilt top on her worktable in order for the photographer to take the pictures for the layout. She'd basted the back and borders together so it would look finished in the photographs. She still had time to do the more intricate quilting stitches before the Expo. With one final kayak lesson, then the kayak trip to follow, things were under control.

She hadn't been able to sleep last night. Visions of a certain handsome opponent kept her tossing and turning. She got up and worked on the Hearts Entwined quilt, hoping to calm her restless energy. Even though her tender wrist made her work slowly, she'd still made progress. She'd been worried about running out of time, but not only would she finish the quilt for the Expo and wrap up the next issue for the magazine, she expected to master the kayaking excursion with ease. She could already visualize how she'd decorate the upstairs office once she won the challenge.

And while she should be excited, she couldn't help but wonder how Ben would handle the decision if he lost. Would he go back to traveling? Leave Tampa behind? Too bad they both couldn't get the promotion.

When the photographer, Dave, arrived, Molly left her office to let him work. She didn't need to hover. Grabbing the new, pink fitted jacket to go with a print blouse and cream skirt, she left her office, motioning for Taylor to meet her in the coffee nook.

"I saw Dave," Taylor said. "You finished the quilt?"

"No. I basted it together for the photos."

"I have to tell you, the women in the office are excited. You've pulled the kayaking gig off while no one has heard a thing about Ben's quilting project. Do you think he ruined it? Maybe he can't face up to losing the challenge."

"Don't get ahead of yourself. Ben is a competitor. If you haven't heard anything, it's because he doesn't want you to hear anything."

Taylor's expression sobered. "He wouldn't play dirty, would he?"

Molly tilted her head, silently saying, "As if?"

"Ohh. That explains why the guys have been so quiet."

"I thought they'd lost interest," Molly quipped. "Especially when Ben disconnected the speaker over his door."

"Hearing Ben's name blared all over the office was beyond annoying, but I doubt the guys forgot. They're just sneaky."

"Look, Ben could have made things difficult for me, but he's been supportive the entire time."

"I don't know . . ."

"I do. Okay, enough chatter. We'd better get back to work."

Taylor's cell phone buzzed. Distracted, she answered, "Hmm. Okay."

Molly chuckled and returned to her office. She spoke to Dave before he left, settled in for a few hours of editing, then her cell phone rang. She snatched it up, reading Second Chances on the caller ID.

"Molly speaking."

"It's Linda. So sorry to bother you, I know you're at work, but we have an emergency."

"What kind of emergency?"

"Tammi called in sick and Mrs. Wilcox from the board of directors is coming in shortly with potential donors. Tammi was supposed to have a presentation and tour all ready. I can handle the tour, but the presentation? I can't even find her notes."

Tammi's bad timing did constitute an emergency. Without new and ongoing support, the center couldn't offer the programs it did.

"When are the donors supposed to arrive?"

"Eleven."

She could take an early lunch, run by the center, and still put in her work hours for the day. "If I come over now, I may be able to find some of the material we've used for previous presentations. Is the center busy?"

"There are a few volunteers here working to make sure the temporary building is in tip-top shape."

"Give me about fifteen minutes."

Molly grabbed her purse and hurried out of her office, stopping long enough to let Taylor know she had an emergency. "I should be back in an hour or so. Cover for me."

"What if something comes up?"

"Just call. I'll get back to you when I can."

She raced to her car and made it to the center in record time. Linda greeted her at the door. "I'm so glad you're here. None of us have ever hosted donors before."

Molly had, plenty of times, since she'd worked with the previous director on more than one occasion. "Anything we can use in Tammi's office?"

"I checked. It's like she never put any material together."

"All right then. Follow me."

When the fire had made moving necessary, Molly remembered storing some of their promotional materials in a storage closet. She hoped she could pull something together last minute.

"Something has to be done about Tammi," Linda commented as they scoured the closet. "We can't have her leaving us high and dry again."

"I'll speak to the board. Let them know they need to talk to her."

"She's past talking to. Moved right into the reprimand stage," Linda huffed. "You know I wouldn't have bothered you, but out of all the volunteers, you seem to have a handle on how the center works."

"I don't mind."

The minutes ticked down to Mrs. Wilcox's arrival. Molly and Linda worked together to pull together stats, testimonials and other information a potential donor would request. Molly set up in the common room, ready for the guests as they walked in the door. After introductions were made, Molly presented a look at Second Chance and why they would be appreciative of any donation or partnering contribution. Once she finished speaking, Linda took over for the tour, leaving Molly alone with Mrs. Wilcox.

"I'm surprised to see you here on a work day."

"I'm on my lunch hour."

"Where is Tammi?"

"Sick, I believe."

"Hmm. This isn't the first time." Mrs. Wilcox frowned. "And from what I've gathered, you've been gracious enough to fill in when needed."

Molly gathered the materials. "I don't mind, but I suppose finding out how committed Tammi is would be a big help."

"I agree. We can't keep calling you away from work." Mrs. Wilcox eyed Molly. "Have you ever considered working here?"

Molly stopped in her tracks. Blinked. "I have a job."

"We'd be lucky to have someone as hardworking and dedicated as you."

"I'm flattered," Molly said. "Thanks, but I'm in the running for a new position with my publisher."

Mrs. Wilcox sighed. "I guess I'll have to get in contact with the other board members."

After Molly had put everything away, she dug her cell phone out of the side pocket of her purse. One missed call. She pulled up her voice mail.

"Get back here as soon as you can," Taylor said, panic in her voice. "Mr. Masterson is back. He wants to meet with you and Ben. I covered for you, but . . . call me."

Molly rushed to her car, speed-dialing Taylor on the way.

"What's up?"

"What's up is Mr. Masterson wants you guys in his office."

"How soon?"

"Fifteen minutes."

Molly ground her teeth together. "On my way." The office was about fifteen minutes away, if traffic didn't slow her down.

Back at the office, she tripped exiting the elevator as she hurried to her office to drop off her purse and take a half dozen deep breaths. With seconds to spare, she took the elevator up one floor and joined Ben as he sat in Mr. Masterson's waiting area.

Ben tossed the magazine he held in his hands on the end table. "Busy today?"

"You could say so." She took a seat beside him. "What's going on now?"

"Don't know. Got a summons just like you."

Great. Their last two visits to the boss's office required both of them doing Masterson's bidding. If he stayed true to form, she didn't think today would be any different.

The door to the office opened and Masterson beckoned them in. "Sorry, phone call I couldn't end." He motioned for them to take a seat. "First, I want to thank you both for attending the Mayoral Awards and accepting my trophy." He shook his head, his eyes merry with amusement. "All these years the mayor has teased me with the award and the year he comes through I'm out of town. Mr. Mayor owes me one."

Molly smiled as she sat, all the while waiting for Mr. Masterson to throw another wrench in the gear.

"But it can be resolved another day." He clasped his hands together. "Molly, tell me more about the Charity Expo."

She blinked. Mr. Masterson had never shown any interest in the Expo before. "It's a way for the community to donate to different charities by bidding on items from local businesses and crafting groups." She pasted a smile on her face while her stomach dipped. What was he up to? "You know I always donate a quilt. This year will be no different."

"Maybe a little."

Her chest grew tight as she recognized his smile meant trouble.

"I'm thinking we should donate the quilt Ben is working on. It'll double the draw of interest for Master's Publishing."

"His . . . quilt?" she sputtered, trying to mask her surprise. A heated flush started up her neck to cover her cheeks. How like Mr. Masterson to use her charity connections for publicity. It was all she could do not to stand up and tell him she didn't appreciate his grandstanding. But she'd look petty and foolish because the bottom line of the Expo was to raise money. Which Mr. Masterson knew how to do.

"You are on target to finish, aren't you Ben?"

"Yes, sir."

"Then it's settled. Molly, get hold of the person in charge and register Ben's quilt."

Mr. Masterson droned on and on but Molly didn't hear a word. All she could think about was his latest move in bringing attention to Ben and bumping her out of contention. Could his support for Ben be any more obvious? Why bother with the challenge at all, if he favored Ben?

Mr. Masterson brought the meeting to a close. "Any money raised goes to great causes, so please, spread the word Master's Publishing is involved." He flashed a winning smile before they left the room. "I say the more the merrier."

Molly held her temper in check until they entered the elevators. When the doors swooshed shut, she spun on Ben. "What was that all about?"

"Since I'm also working on a quilt, he must have thought additional publicity from Master's Publishing would benefit the Expo."

"More like benefit Master's Publishing." She frowned. "Stuff like this isn't on his radar. How did he come up with the idea?"

Ben grimaced. "I might have mentioned the idea to him."

"Might have?"

"Okay, I did mention it."

"Why would you say anything in the first place?"

"I was thinking ahead, in light of the competition." He ran a hand through his hair. "You took to kayaking like a pro. Then you were all over the newspaper after the awards ceremony. I didn't want you to get the best of me so I mentioned the idea." His troubled gaze met hers. "It all happened before I realized supporting charities isn't a game to you."

"Mr. Masterson does these things to get publicity," she fumed. "And you didn't dissuade him since my quilt will be featured?"

He held his hands up. "What was I supposed to do? Disagree with the boss? It was my idea. Besides, I like the idea of helping."

"This is crazy."

"It's competition. I warned you I didn't like things easy."

"Silly of me to have forgotten." She turned away from him and crossed her arms over her chest. Bile churned in her stomach. How could he one up her like he did? She thought they'd moved beyond being rivals. Thought there might be a deeper connection between them. How wrong could she be? It all came back to the job promotion.

"Where were you earlier?"

"Out." No way would she tell him and have the information leak back to Mr. Masterson. No more getting chummy with the enemy—as she now viewed him. The door slid open on their floor and she stormed out.

"Molly, wait."

"I have work to do, Ben," she called over her shoulder. She marched on, trying to simmer down before she said or did something she'd regret.

⁂

When Ben got back to his office, he slammed the door behind him and paced the room, kicking the golf bag in the corner as he passed by.

When he'd mentioned the Expo idea to Masterson, he didn't think it would go anywhere. At the time, he just wanted to keep one step ahead of Molly. Who knew she'd turn into a formidable opponent? He hadn't, so he'd regrouped. Thought up other options to keep him in the forefront of both his boss and the competition. If he'd known Molly's passion for charity work, he never would have horned in.

Her passion for helping others was one of the things he admired about her, one among a growing list of attributes. By spending time with her, Ben found himself wanting to contribute as well. He allowed himself to look beyond the job confines of his life, which had been all he had going on, to focus on others. Wasn't getting involved in the community one of the things he wanted to do when he settled down? Until the challenge, he had no idea how or what to do. Molly's influence had him rethinking his priorities.

A brief knock sounded on the door. Charlie stuck his head in the office. "So, how'd it go?"

"Just like you thought. Masterson liked the idea of donating my quilt to the Charity Expo."

"And Molly?" he asked as he entered the room.

"She didn't like it but went along. Gotta hand it to her, she wasn't happy, but played along like a pro."

"You're not getting soft, are you?"

Soft? If soft meant being considerate, of considering Molly's feelings first, then, yeah, he must be. "I just wish there was a way neither of us had to win or lose."

"There is no other way. It's called life."

"When did you get so cynical?"

Charlie's eyes went flinty cold as he faced Ben. "I just want to see you get the job. Molly understands. This is business."

Did she? There was no denying the hurt in her eyes when Masterson laid out his plan.

"Look, you've almost finished the quilt," Charlie told him as he opened the door on his way out. "Molly has the kayak trip on the weekend. By next week, you'll be editor-in-chief. Keep your eyes on the prize, buddy."

The door closed, leaving Ben in silence.

When had Charlie become so annoying? Didn't the guy realize there was more at stake here than the job? Even though he'd started out with the promotion on his mind, getting to know Molly and her friends had shown him life beyond the job. Relationships were important and he didn't want to lose what he'd started with Molly. Once Masterson made his selection for editor-in-chief, they'd sit down and figure out their relationship.

Still, he didn't like the accusing look on Molly's face. Like he'd betrayed her. It hadn't felt like it at the time. He'd been moving things along in the spirit of the competition. But what seemed natural to him didn't sit well with Molly. She was up-front and honest. He'd handled his part in the challenge badly. He realized it didn't all come down to winning.

Instead of working, Ben continued to pace his office. By late afternoon, he had enough questions running through his head to last for hours. He left his office and strode to Molly's, ready to hash out their differences. He'd just reached for the doorknob when Taylor stopped him.

"She's not there."

"Where is she?"

"I don't know. She left."

Ben stared at the door.

"She seemed upset after your meeting upstairs."

"She told you?"

"No, but I can see what's going on."

Concerned friend or office gossip? With the challenge coming close to the end and sides being drawn, he shouldn't be surprised if all information was fair game. But Taylor's distress mirrored Molly's.

"I didn't mean to hurt her," he said.

"Maybe not, but you did just the same."

"How can I make it up to her?"

"Ben, you have to understand. Molly goes after things differently than you. If you wanted to put your quilt in the Expo, she would have been glad to arrange it. But you blindsided her. I get you want to win the challenge, but at what cost?"

What cost indeed. For both of them.

He intended to return to his office but, on a hunch, detoured to the elevator and the vacant office upstairs. The office he'd come to think of as his own.

He entered, hoping to find Molly here, angry and ready to rectify the mess he'd created. An empty room greeted him. No Molly in sight. He strode to the window, jammed his hands in his slacks pockets, and stared outside.

Another picture-perfect spring day in Tampa. The bright sun and clear blue skies were almost too bright. For a moment, he had a fanciful thought of the city as his for the taking. Masterson had become successful with that attitude. Why not Ben?

Molly's face flashed in his mind, her face taut with shock, then hurt. He closed his eyes, instead envisioning her generous smile and sparkle of life. That Molly would have laughed with him before he messed up.

He opened his eyes, gazing at the vista before him. Before their rivalry ended, he'd find a way to make her happy again.

12

Molly sat on the dock jutting over the lake, her bare feet dangling over the placid water. Her shorts and T-shirt were still damp from her last kayaking lesson. Once finished, Paul had pronounced her ready to take on any adventure she set her mind to. She should be happy, but her heart missed the memo. Time to skedaddle, but couldn't shake her lethargy. She had work from the office waiting for her at home, and hoped to get in a few hours of work on the quilt. But she sat there, unable to work up the energy to do either.

Paul had just taken off for parts unknown. Molly chuckled. Her coach until the end, just like he promised. She'd probably looked as downcast as she felt, because he'd asked what was up with her. She shrugged him off, using her workload as an excuse. She didn't think he believed her, but didn't push the issue. When Molly lugged the kayak to the shed, he asked if she wanted to grab dinner, but she declined, deciding to hang out here to watch the sun set.

The sky had turned a brilliant streak of orange and yellow during her lesson. Now, darker shades of blue and purple melded as the sun sank toward the horizon. Activity on the lake had grown quiet, with boaters having retired for the day. An insect buzzed by, breaking the silence, but not Molly's troubled thoughts.

How could she have been so wrong about Ben? She thought they were getting closer, in a romantic way. He seemed to care about her, but was it all an act to throw her off guard? And how would she face him at work? Could he still be hatching up ideas to make him valuable in their boss's estimation?

She removed her glasses to rub her weary eyes. Feeling sorry for herself, she'd reverted back to the old comfortable standby. How silly of her to think Ben might be attracted to her. Like contacts would make a difference. At Nora's house, when she thought he might kiss her, her hopes had soared. When he did kiss her, she moved one step closer to love. And as much as she wanted him to, now a part of her wondered about his motivation. It had been so long since she'd liked a guy enough to risk getting involved. And then he had to go and change the rules on her.

All the women in the office still had high hopes Molly would win the challenge. She snorted. Stupid idea. If anything, his latest tactic should get her competitive spirit going, but instead the opposite happened. She wanted to hole up in her apartment to quilt or read. Not deal with reality or obsess over the idea Ben had used their attraction against her.

Lord, I did it again. Hoped for something out of my reach.

A car door slammed, but she didn't bother to look over her shoulder and check it out. Probably Jed, heading home to his wife and family after his last lesson of the day.

She leaned back, resting her palms on the rough wood behind her, enjoying the quiet. Until the sound of footsteps sounded on the dock.

She sat up, wiping her hands, thinking she'd leave whoever had arrived some privacy. She turned her head, surprised to see her mother.

"Mom. What are you doing here?"

Her mother stopped beside her, uncertainty lining her face. "Paul told me you had your last lesson tonight. I wanted to see how you were doing."

"You could have called me."

Her mother took a seat beside Molly. "I could have, but I wanted to see you in person."

"To make sure I'm still in one piece?" she asked with bitterness.

"I deserved that." Her mother gazed out over the water. "Paul has been giving me updates, so I know you're just fine. Better than fine, according to him."

"It has been great having him around."

The older woman hesitated. "It should never have come to this."

"To what?"

"You and your brother having a strained relationship because of me."

Molly shrugged. "You were always proud of him. I understood."

"And I've always been proud of you too, Molly."

She almost snorted, but decided not to be rude. "It's never seemed that way to me."

"Because I never showed it."

Molly glanced at her, but said nothing. Waited. *You got the ball rolling, Mom. Now finish.*

Her mom took a breath. "When you were younger, I guess I just didn't know how to deal with a sickly child. Your brother had always been healthy, so I didn't have to worry about him."

"I know."

"I don't think you do." She paused, as if searching for the right words. "It all started when you were two years old. We were at a church picnic when some sort of bug bit you. At first, I noticed a small welt and didn't think it worth worrying about. We stayed at the picnic an hour longer. By the time we got home, the welt had grown to twice its size, turning red and hot to the touch.

"I applied some over-the-counter cream, but your breathing started growing labored. Your father bundled us up in the car to drive to the emergency room. Sure enough, you'd had a severe reaction."

"I don't remember."

"You were fussy and whining until the medicine the doctor prescribed settled you down. I rocked you for hours, praying you wouldn't die. Time passed and your breathing became steady again. We'd passed the danger point. Afterward, you seemed to be more susceptible to . . . everything"

Silence fell between them.

"Molly, I've always been overprotective because I was scared. After the trip to the hospital I wondered, what if something happened to you again? What if I let you down by not properly taking care of you the next time you had a reaction? I worried so much, I made myself numb with fear. I let a distance form between us, thinking if we weren't close, if something horrible happened to you, it wouldn't hurt so badly."

"I never knew."

"Because I never told you."

Molly nearly laughed out loud. She'd grown up keeping her distance from people, a lesson she'd learned from her mother. All these years she'd had the power to change her destiny, if she'd known the truth behind her mother's actions.

Instead, Nora and friends had surrounded her with love when she needed it most. If not, she would never have had the confidence in her job or been able to volunteer at Second Chances.

"It's okay, Mom. I don't expect anything from you."

"But you should." Her voice caught. "I'm your mother. And though I haven't shown it, I do love you."

The words she'd always wanted to hear. Too little, too late?

"Do you believe me?"

She wanted to. She truly wanted to.

Molly watched the tears in her mother's eyes trickle down her cheeks. After all these years, she saw real emotion reflected there. Real love. She knew what it looked like because she'd seen it in Nora's eyes over the years.

Molly's chest hitched. "Why are you telling me now?"

"I've wanted to tell you for a long time, but the distance between us grew wider and you were so busy with your job and activities." Her mother blew out a breath. "I didn't know how to bridge the gap."

"But at your house, when I told you about the kayaking challenge, you weren't supportive."

"I fell back on old patterns. I worried about me, not what was good for you. But as I tried to talk you out of it, for the first time, I saw determination in your eyes, Molly. You were going to participate, no matter what your father and I said."

She folded her hands in her lap. "Paul told us how wrong we were about you. You wanted the position at work and you were going after it no matter the cost. He told us you had real Henderson grit and we needed to respect that."

"It's more than grit," Molly realized. "It has to do with my relationship with God. I can do all things through Christ who strengthens me."

Her mother nodded. "You've more than proved it. We let our relationship with Christ lapse while yours grew stronger."

Molly hoped her parents would search out God as she had.

"Your father and I talked for hours after you left. Paul was right. I'm the one with no grit. If I had, I'd never have let my fears influence my relationship with you. With our entire family. Molly, you've grown up to be a very capable, very loving young woman. I let Nora handle all the emotional entanglements in your life and because of it, I missed out on sharing memories with my own daughter." She swallowed her tears. "I can't tell you how sorry I am."

Molly digested her mother's words. Couldn't deny the longing in her heart. "So are you telling me you want a do-over?"

"I know we can't go back. I can't change decisions I've made, but we can start anew." Her mother paused again, love and uncertainty reflected in her eyes. "Can you forgive me, Molly?"

Could she? Her heart beat faster. She'd waited her whole life for this conversation.

The next step fell to her. Accept her mother's faults and attempt at reconciliation, or turn her back on the woman who had just bared her soul. There was only one correct choice to make.

"I forgive you." She took her mother's hand in hers. "We have a lot of catching up to do, Mom."

Her mother started to laugh between her tears, hugging her daughter. "I thought for sure you'd tell me there was no going back."

"There's always a chance to start over."

They talked until the sun set and stars sparkled in the dark sky, nowhere near caught up on the lost years, but knowing with a fresh start, they had the promise of making new memories.

As they walked to their cars, her mom asked, "How is the challenge at work going?"

Molly groaned. "You had to bring up the one topic sure to ruin our good time."

"I'm sorry," her mother said, tensing as if she'd said something wrong again.

"No, it's okay. You didn't know." Molly paused by her car to update her mother about the latest developments.

"Molly, I can't believe you're letting Ben get the best of you."

"He doesn't like things to be easy."

"Then you just have to show him his tricks will not affect you. Finish the quilt. Be proud of what you've accomplished. I have no doubt your creation will be the bigger draw at the Expo."

"I hope."

"You should be judged on your work merit, not how much publicity you garner for the publisher."

"From your mouth," she muttered.

Her mother pulled her into a hug. "Go after what you want, Molly."

From the beginning, Molly knew her boss's motivation behind the challenge was for show. Yet, she still wanted the job. But first, she had to get back on track. Finish the quilt. Get through the kayak trip.

"Thanks, Mom."

Her mother brushed a stray strand of Molly's hair from her cheek. "You can win."

And with her mother's newfound support, the support she'd always prayed for, Molly believed she could.

Tuesday morning, Molly arrived at the office, full of renewed energy. Her mother's pep talk had gone a long way in knocking her out of her funk over Ben.

She'd dressed in a simple pink sheath dress and matching open-toe pumps. Not her usual office attire, but hey, why shouldn't she try something different? Hair pulled back and contacts in place, she marched to her office as if she didn't have a care in the world.

Last night she'd started stitching the back of the quilt to the quilt top, the final task in completing the project. The embroidery stitch she'd decided on wasn't too elaborate, so she planned on completing the entire project in time for the Expo. In the meantime, she'd come up with an idea to one-up Ben.

"Do you remember I told you Ben and I are to write an article to chronicle our parts in the challenge?" she asked as she approached Taylor's desk.

"Yes." Taylor typed a command on her computer keyboard then turned her attention to Molly.

"Well, Nora told me Ben is stopping by her house this morning to finish the quilt."

"And . . . ?"

"I asked our photographer to stop by and get some pictures of Ben attempting needlework."

Taylor chuckled. "He *is* the one who wants publicity."

"Exactly."

"This battle is the best thing to happen in the office in a long time. Who knew work could be so entertaining?"

Molly curtsied. "We aim to please at Master's Publishing."

Taylor tilted her head as she regarded her friend. "You continue to amaze me."

"Well, Ben has made it known he doesn't like easy. His wish is my command."

Jumping up from her seat, Taylor gave Molly a quick hug. "You are so going to win."

"Been my plan all along."

At her desk, Molly dug into her workload. An hour later, she ventured to the coffee nook for a refill. On her way back to her office, Ben stopped her, looking suave in navy slacks and a tan button-down shirt.

"Really?"

She fought to hide her smile but knew she didn't succeed.

"You sent Dave to take pictures?"

She shrugged. "You and Mr. Masterson are all about the publicity. Just my way of helping the cause."

"I don't need publicity. Now donations for both our quilts, there's another story."

"Your latest play did catch me off guard."

"Look, I know you're upset, but the bottom line is we're both contributing to a good cause."

"True. And the proof will be available for all to see when I add pictures of you, hard at work, to the article I'm submitting to Mr. Masterson."

"Aren't you afraid I'll retaliate? Face it, pictures of me sewing are nothing compared to you in your kayak gear, drenched to the bone."

"You wouldn't dare."

"And why not?"

"Because you're a decent guy and you wouldn't want to humiliate me."

"What about my humiliation?"

"Consider taking one for the team."

Ben opened his mouth, but before he could speak, eavesdropping Charlie refilled his coffee mug. "We could send Dave to take pictures of you on your kayak run. It's not too late."

"You could, but he's busy Saturday."

"And how do you know?"

Taylor joined the group. "Because we booked him."

Charlie frowned. "For what?"

"A big craft fair at the fairgrounds."

Ben grinned at Molly. "Clever."

Molly blew on her fingertips, then brushed them on her shoulder. "What can I say? I've learned from the best."

"Is that a compliment?"

"Did I say who I learned from? It could have been my brother."

"Or maybe she's just sneaky," Taylor added.

"Or afraid she's going to lose," Charlie threw into the mix.

Taylor spun on him, slamming her hands on her hips. "You have no idea what you're talking about. She's way ahead of Ben."

"And you know this how?"

"Because she's a good employee, a top-notch editor, and a good person."

Charlie snorted. "Right, like it matters. Ben, here, is just as good at his job, and he's got television credit to boot. Masterson is gonna be all over Ben's expertise to promote his new magazine."

Molly's good mood deflated at those words. Of course, Ben's credentials were working in his favor. Even if he were the worst editor ever, which he was not. Her little stunt may have stirred the competitive waters at the office, but it didn't change the fact Molly limped in like the underdog.

"We work for a magazine, not television," Taylor huffed. "Have you forgotten, Charlie?"

"And this is a challenge, Taylor. Ready to admit defeat?"

"Enough, children." Ben glanced at Molly. "We've created monsters."

"Speak for yourself. I've created friends."

She knew her words hit the intended mark when Ben's face went blank. At his reaction, her mind went numb. Why on earth had she said those unkind words? Because he riled her competitive spirit? Not a good enough reason.

Guilt gnawed at her. How could she take what he'd told her in confidence and throw it back at him?

Ben stepped into her personal space, his face close to hers. "We're far from over."

She shivered, both from his words and the fact he stood so close she could feel his body heat. Okay, the shivering came more from the intense expression he focused on her.

"Only a few days left," she reminded him, her voice so low and husky she barely recognized it. She took a step back. "Then we'll find out who moves up to the new office."

"Be prepared to lose."

Molly couldn't read his closed expression, but knew it meant big trouble. He turned on his heel and strode back to his desk, leaving Molly torn between apologizing for her words or letting it go.

Remorse smacked her again. She hadn't meant to be mean, but as the clock ran out, the stakes brought out the worst out in everyone.

"You two are delusional," Charlie added his final volley before walking away.

Molly sighed. "How pleasant."

"Hey. Don't feel bad. Ben deserved payback."

"I don't play these games, Taylor."

"Just hang in there. Next week, you'll have the answer."

Whether she liked it or not.

As they walked to Taylor's desk, she said, "Mr. Masterson has always been fair."

"Even though Ben has the obvious advantage?" No matter how Molly analyzed the state of the battle, she couldn't find a downside for Ben.

"Obvious to whom? Mr. Masterson will do what is best for the magazine, no matter who is the most successful in his challenge."

"True, despite his tactics," Molly agreed. Then remembered her unkind words. "I should talk to Ben."

Taylor took hold of her arm. "Let him cool off, Molly."

"You're right."

The afternoon flew by as Molly worked, but she couldn't stop revisiting the scene with Ben and how she'd lashed out at him. The more she thought about it, the more restless she became, traveling back and forth for coffee three more times in the afternoon. Unusual for her, since she had two cups, tops, in the morning. But then, her life had been topsy-turvy for a while now, so why should it be so surprising she'd drink more coffee than usual?

At five, she tidied her desk, gathered material she needed to pass off to Taylor and packed her belongings before heading out. She picked up her tote, looking inside to make sure she'd packed all her quilting supplies.

"That's weird."

She had tucked the Hearts Entwined quilt in her tote bag after lunch, but now it was gone. She didn't remember taking it out at any point during the afternoon. Dropping the tote, she searched the office, first around the worktable, then around her desk. She opened desk drawers. Looked behind the chair. Under the desk. Panic set in when she couldn't find the quilt anywhere. She opened the door, nearly running into Taylor as she raced out.

"Whoa. What's your hurry?"

"Taylor, do you have the quilt?"

She frowned. "No. Why?"

"I can't find it. Did Dave take it for more pictures?"

"I haven't seen him all afternoon."

"Then where could it be?"

"Wait. Are you saying you've misplaced it?"

Molly groaned in response.

"Did you take it out of the office to work on it?"

Molly shook her head. "No. It's been in my tote bag all afternoon." She frowned. "Or at least I thought it was."

Taylor searched around her own desk. "It's not here. And it's too big to miss." She glanced at Molly. "Did anyone stop by your office?"

"No. Besides, how could I possibly miss someone leaving my office with the quilt?" She rubbed her temples. "Did you notice anyone?"

"No. But I did meet you at the coffee nook a couple times this afternoon. Anyone could have walked into your office and we wouldn't have noticed."

Molly's heart sank. "But who would want it? It's not like . . ."

And then it hit her. She turned on her heel and beelined directly to Ben's office. Without knocking, she burst through the door. "Very funny. Now hand it over."

He looked up from the computer screen. "Hand over what?"

"I get turnabout is fair play, but I'm serious, Ben. Give me the quilt."

A wrinkle marred his brow. "The one you've been working on for the magazine?"

"What else would it be, yes, the one for the magazine."

Ben stood. "Molly, I don't have it."

"Right." She began to walk around his desk. "And you're not all about the competition."

He stepped out of her way. "Honestly, I don't have it."

Molly stopped searching for a moment and noticed the confusion on his face.

"You didn't come to my office and swipe the quilt?"

"Why would I?"

"Payback for having your picture taken."

"You think I'd stoop to a childish prank?"

She threw up her hands. "I don't know what to think. All I know is the quilt, and all my hours of work, is missing."

He rounded the desk to stand before her. "Molly, I didn't take it. I know how much the quilt means to you."

"Then who would?"

13

Ben and Molly tore up his office looking for the quilt. He'd never seen Molly so upset. Not that he blamed her. After all the hours spent working on the project, she deserved to be a wreck.

"This cannot be happening," she kept repeating.

"Molly, we'll find it," he reassured her. Even to himself he sounded unsure.

"Because we've been successful so far?"

"There has to be a logical explanation."

"Like what?"

He ran a hand through his hair. "I don't know. I'm thinking."

"I have to find it, Ben." Her voice choked, breaking his heart. "The deadline is right around the corner."

"I know. Keep looking."

But still, they came up empty.

"You don't think Mr. Masterson would have taken it?"

"He doesn't get involved in our projects."

"Even to sabotage the challenge?"

"Molly, that's a stretch. Even for him."

She made a three-sixty of the room and smacked her palm against her forehead. "Upstairs," she said, running to the elevator.

"What are you thinking?"

"The empty office. The one we're both working toward."

He didn't see how an office tied in, but right now, they were grasping at straws.

Molly stabbed at the elevator button on the journey of one floor.

"Impatience won't make it go any faster."

She stopped. "Sorry. Nervous energy."

Once in the office, Ben flipped on the lights. Molly ran straight to the desk, pulling open the drawers.

"Nothing." She sagged against the desk. "Nothing."

"Did you think you'd find it here?"

"I'd hoped."

He glanced at his watch. "Let me check with Masterson. He might still be here."

Molly grabbed his arm to stop him. "No. Ben, if he finds out what is going on it'll ruin everything."

"I'll ask his secretary. Wait here."

She waved him off, pacing the office as he left.

Ben caught Masterson's secretary just as she was leaving for the day, but she knew nothing about a quilt. Masterson hadn't mentioned anything about it either.

"He doesn't have it," Ben informed Molly when he returned. He strode to the windows where she stood, stepping close to her. "His secretary doesn't know anything."

"I can't believe it's gone."

He heard the tremor in her voice, and when he looked at her, his stomach clenched. Tears rolled down her cheeks. "What am I going to do?" she whispered.

Right then and there, the challenge didn't mean a thing to Ben. Not at the expense of Molly's well-being. He pulled her into his embrace. She went rigid at first, then gave into her emotions and melted against his chest. He rocked her in his arms as she sobbed, burying his nose in her sweet-smelling hair, keeping his own emotions in check.

After a time, her crying slowed and she pulled away from him, wiping her face.

"Molly, I—"

"There's nothing to say, Ben."

"Tomorrow, when all the staff is here, we'll find out what's going on."

"What's going on is I lost the quilt."

"You didn't lose it, Molly."

"It's not like it got up and walked away."

"I told you, there's got to be a sensible reason."

"And in the meantime?" She swiped at her damp cheeks again. "I have two weeks until the Expo. I don't think I can make another quilt in time."

"You could try. Ask Nora and the ladies."

"Even if I could, I don't think I have enough fabric left from my readers. I already used most of the material. Without the donations, I have no story."

Ben never felt so helpless in his life. It wasn't like he could go to the referee and cry foul. There were no game book rules for him to fall back on.

"We'll find it, Molly."

Her shoulders drooped. "Wishful thinking, Ben."

⁂

The following morning, after a sleepless night, Molly dragged into work, having thrown on an oversized shirt and slacks. She'd gathered the remaining fabric pieces from her readers to see how much she had left to start a new quilt. Not as much as when she began the project, but enough if she added remnants she'd collected from her previous projects. The question was, could she finish it in time? She'd started cutting new pattern pieces, ready to take each day one step at a time until she completed quilt number two.

When she got settled in at her desk, she noticed a note from Ben, asking her to stop by his office. Not thrilled at having to face him after her meltdown last night, she squared her shoulders and marched to his office. How humiliating he should see her at her emotional worst.

When he'd pulled her into his embrace, she'd been stunned by how right it felt. Like she had a right to go to him for comfort any time she needed it. Soon, the tears had overtaken her and all she could do was hold on and ride out the storm. What must he think of her now? A woman who couldn't deal with a catastrophe, because losing the quilt sure constituted as one.

She shook her head to get rid of her melancholy. They still had to work together. She'd suck up her embarrassment and act like the professional she wanted everyone in the office to see.

She knocked on Ben's door and popped her head inside. "You wanted to see me?"

"C'mon in." He rose and circled the desk, motioning for her to take a seat in the chair before his desk. He sat back against the desk, ankles crossed, arms folded over his chest.

The intensity of his gaze nearly undid her. "How are you?"

She squirmed in the seat. "I've been better."

"I figured." He hesitated for a moment, before his take-charge attitude took over.

"I spoke to Nora and the ladies last night."

Oh great, here it comes.

"They want to help you put together a new quilt."

"I'll handle it, Ben."

"Nora predicted you'd say that. And while I can appreciate your stubborn streak, I have learned one important thing since coming back to Tampa. We all need people in our lives. A support group, if you will."

"I have all the support I need. If I wanted their help, I'd have asked them."

"Why are you being so difficult?"

"Because the quilt went missing on my watch." She rose and started pacing to get her temper under control. "I'm not trying to be difficult, Ben. Maybe you can't understand, but this is *my* project. It has been from the moment I came up with the idea. I promised my readers I would be the one sewing the quilt. Not my friends. Not my coworkers. Me."

"Ok, I get you made a promise to your readers. But come on, you have to be realistic. Even if you could pull a quilt together in a short time, you'd have to do it at the expense of everything else in your life."

"You think I haven't considered the ramifications?"

"I don't know what is going on in your head."

She halted before him while trying to think of a way to make her point in a way he'd understand. "Have you made a connection with your readers, Ben? On a personal level?"

"Not like you."

She began to prowl the office again. "Your relationship with your readers is different. I've been the editor and written articles for *Quilter's Heart* so the women know me. They've seen the types of quilts I've created over the years. Read about the festivals I've attended around the country. I've shared new products with them. Bonded with the women. When I put a call out for personal letters to explain the fabric choices they sent in, I received more mail than I ever expected. After reading their testimonies, I can relate with so many of these women, admire even more."

She noticed his perplexed look and leaned against the desk right next to him. "Let me put it in a way you can relate to. If you were on a sports team, say a baseball team, and you lost the only ball for the game, wouldn't you feel personally responsible?"

"Sure, but—"

"I dropped the ball, Ben. I lost the quilt."

"Wait. Back up. You didn't lose anything."

She began to pace again, hoping he'd understand where she stood on the matter of making the new quilt. She reached the corner of the room, ready to turn in the opposite direction when her gaze lit on a bright color on the dark carpet just beside his golf bag. A sense of heaviness settled over her as she bent down to discover a snippet of fabric. Fabric just like one of the red pieces she'd used in the missing quilt.

Her stomach sank as she held it up a trembling hand for Ben to see. "Care to explain?"

He frowned. "I have no idea."

"It's a piece of the quilt."

"Not possible."

She got down on her hands and knees to search the room again. By the golf bag. Under and around his desk. She found two additional swatches of material under the trash basket. She sat back on her heels, holding them up.

Ben looked as shocked as she felt.

"Molly, I swear. I don't know where those came from."

"Am I supposed to believe you?" She shook the fabric pieces in her hand.

His face went hard and unyielding. "I'm telling you the truth. Whoever took the quilt is making it look like I'm involved."

"Well, I see another ploy to get my focus off the challenge so you can win the promotion."

"You think I would stoop this low?"

"I lost all sense of reality when the quilt went missing" She rose on unsteady legs. He reached out to help her, but she shook him off. She headed to the door to get away from him, needing fresh air to clear her mind and calm her racing heart.

Ben stopped her before she could escape. "Mark my words, Molly. I'm going to find out what is going on and prove you are wrong about me."

Then he moved out of the way as she fled the room, feeling the full weight of his steady gaze on her retreating back.

———

By Friday night, Molly couldn't wait for the weekend to start. She had to resort to using the sewing machine to piece together half of the quilt top. When her part in the kayaking challenge ended tomorrow, she'd have time to devote more hours to finishing the quilt.

She hadn't spoken to Ben since the scene in his office, avoiding him at every move. She didn't trust herself to keep from lashing out at him.

She went through the motions, but couldn't keep her mind focused on any one thing. She worried about the quilt, her job, the kids she'd be kayaking with. What a mess. But in the forefront, she couldn't keep her mind from circling back to Ben.

Would he sink so low? He insisted he'd been framed, but how convenient.

She finally called it quits and went to bed. After tossing and turning for hours, she concluded she'd fallen hard for the guy who might have sabotaged her career. Might, being the operative word.

When Ben first came to work at Master's Publishing, she wouldn't have had any problem believing he took the quilt to make her look bad. But since then, especially these past few weeks, she'd come to know him. And the Ben she'd come to know and like would never pull a cheap stunt. Or comfort her in the way he did while her world fell apart. As much as she appreciated his comfort, it still didn't explain the fabric in his office or the fact the quilt hadn't turned up.

She'd flipped onto her back to stare at the ceiling, mentally crabbing about her bad choice in men.

She'd let her guard down around Ben, thinking he might be different. He'd touched her life in a special way, with his concern, his humor and willingness to help her at a moment's notice. It would be a long time, if ever, before she got over him.

But still, as much as the evidence she found in Ben's office put him in a bad light, it was no proof he'd taken the quilt. And knowing how much he loved sports, she couldn't imagine him wanting to win the challenge on anything less than an honorable note. So why couldn't she give him the benefit of the doubt?

Sometime after three a.m., she'd fallen asleep. Dead to the world, a heavy knocking outside shook her from her sleep. Startled, it took her a few seconds to figure out the pounding came from her door. She heard a muffled, "Molly," when it registered someone wanted in.

"Coming, coming," she muttered as she rolled from the bed, groggy and disoriented. She pulled back the deadbolt and pulled open the door.

"You're late," her brother informed her.

"What?"

"The kayaking trip? With the teenagers?"

She blinked, then his words hit her. "What time is it?"

"Nine. You're already a half-hour late."

"Why didn't you call me?"

"I did. Went straight to voice mail."

"Give me a minute," she said, racing to her bedroom to throw on T-shirt and shorts.

"A minute is all the time you have," he called after her.

She ran a brush through her scary hair, splashed water on her face, and ran the toothbrush over her teeth before hurrying back into the living room. "Let's go."

She grabbed her keys and followed Paul out the door to the truck. "The kayak?"

"Already at the river." He put the truck in gear, then shot her a worried look. "How could you forget?"

"It's been a horrible week."

He drove out of the apartment complex, before saying in a somber tone, "I heard about the quilt."

She stopped in the act of pulling her hair into a ponytail. "You did?"

"People are worried about you."

She didn't want to know who the people were. Bad enough she had an entire office that pitied her. "I was up all night working on the new quilt. I forgot to set my alarm."

"How's the quilt coming along?"

"Slow."

Stopping at a red light, Paul sent her a fierce coach stare. "I get you're consumed with the quilt right now, but try to get your mind in the challenge. If there even is one once we get to the river."

"If your speech was meant to fire me up, it's not working."

"Think of Sabrina."

That worked.

He drove through Saturday morning traffic, getting them to the river in no time. He peeled into the parking lot and cut off the engine. They both jumped from the truck at once, running to the river's edge. Hers was the lone kayak in sight.

Taylor came to her side. "They had to get started without you."

Molly grabbed a paddle. "I can still make time."

Taylor grabbed her arm to stop her. "You can, but Mr. Masterson will know you came late."

Her friend tilted her head over her shoulder. Molly looked, catching a glimpse of Charlie and a few other guys from the office. Yeah, Mr. Masterson would soon know she screwed up.

"I don't care. I can't let the kids down," she said as she donned her protective gear.

Once she had everything in place, she started to drag the kayak to the water. When it moved with ease, she figured Paul had grabbed hold of the other end to set the boat into the water. She turned to thank him, meeting Ben's intense gaze instead. After letting go of his end, he stood there, silent.

"I bet you're loving this."

"Then you'd be wrong."

"You got the job, Ben. No point hanging around."

"We don't know for sure."

She lowered herself into the boat. "Sure, we do." She pushed off from the bank and began paddling, keeping her stokes steady in hopes of reaching the group. It took her a while, but she soon reached Sabrina.

"Glad you could make it," the teen said, her face sulky.

"I am so sorry."

"Save it."

"I messed up, Sabrina. But I'm here."

"I thought we were in this together."

"We are. Once I realized how late it was, I could have blown off the trip and not shown up. But I came because of you."

"More like for your job. I saw all your friends here."

"The job doesn't matter. I'm sure I've lost the promotion."

Sabrina's face softened. "You came, anyway."

"Yes. I told you we'd beat those boys. Well, maybe not now, but at least you're not alone."

After a few minutes of paddling, Sabrina chatted away. Molly knew the girl wasn't mad at her any longer. She blew out a breath, working the paddle to keep a steady pace. A little farther ahead, Sabrina's crush, Mark, waited for her while his buddy Jason paddled ahead.

"Somebody has a crush," she teased Sabrina.

"It's weird. Ever since the day we had the water fight, he's been talking to me."

"He needed an excuse to get your attention. I assume he has it?"

The girl grinned. "Oh, yeah."

Molly chuckled. She recognized the smitten expression on Sabrina's face. She'd imagined she'd worn it a time or two whenever she thought about Ben.

She couldn't imagine why he'd shown up, unless he wanted to gloat. Which he didn't do. No, his eyes had been heavy with concern. For her.

She shoved the paddle into the water, releasing all the frustration bottled up inside her. Between the quilt, the challenge, disappointing the women in the office, and thinking about Ben, she worked out her stress by throwing her energy into every stroke of the paddle.

She and Sabrina were the last to make it to the take-out spot, but when they arrived, a loud cheer went up from the crowd who greeted them. Molly rolled her eyes. Why on earth they were applauding she had no idea, but Sabrina smiled and lapped up the attention. Molly enjoyed it for her, especially when Sabrina turned to Mark and Jason and stuck her tongue out in true teenage fashion, as if to say, So There.

She wanted to pull the same tactic with Ben, but she'd lost her chance when she overslept.

On dry land again, Molly thanked everyone for coming, even as she apologized for arriving late. To her surprise, no one thought less of her. Instead, they congratulated her for showing up.

Her mother pulled her aside, wrapping Molly in a solid hug. "You were great. Got in the boat and took off down the river like a pro."

Molly pulled back and blew a strand of hair from her eyes. "Between the lessons and Paul's support, I surprised myself."

Her mother frowned. "Paul told me about your quilt. I'm so sorry."

"I had some fabric left over so I'm piecing together a new quilt."

"Did you ever find out how it went missing?"

Molly shook her head. "No. It's still a mystery."

"Let me know if you need anything. Even company while you work."

Her heart shifted in her chest. "Thanks, Mom. I will."

Her father came over to give her another hug. As her parents made their way to the parking lot and the remainder of the crowd dispersed, Molly went to help Paul move the kayak to the truck. Taylor stopped her. "Give me the end."

"Thanks."

As the two worked together, Molly noticed the looks her brother and friend exchanged.

"Okay, you two. What's going on?"

Taylor blushed a becoming shade of pink.

Molly turned to her brother. "So Taylor is the reason you've been running off to your secretive plans?"

Paul winked. Now she knew how her brother learned about the quilt going missing. Taylor.

"So you've been keeping my brother informed about events at the office?"

"Guilty."

"I knew you had a crush on him, but when did you two get together?"

Paul sauntered over and threw his good arm around Taylor's shoulder. "She called me the same day you stopped by the folks' to ask me to be your coach."

"You knew all along?"

"No," Taylor rushed to say. "I didn't think you'd actually call him, so I decided to intervene on your behalf. When he told me you had called, I pretended to be following up, but didn't spill the beans." She glanced up at Paul and her face softened. "We started talking and the next thing I knew, he asked me out."

Molly poked Paul's arm with her elbow. "Smooth."

"What can I say, Taylor is pretty, smart, and a good friend to my sister. The total package."

"I'm happy for both of you." She grimaced. "At least you have your lives under control."

"So will you, Sis. Try not to worry."

Right. Easier said than done.

She glanced around. No Ben. He hadn't driven to the next access point to throw the latest disaster in her face. Probably busy collecting boxes to move his stuff to the office upstairs, she thought. Now she understood why people hated to lose a competition. It stunk.

Soon, Paul had her in the truck and dropped her off at the apartment. She took a shower, made a sandwich, intending to spend the remainder of the day working on the quilt. She'd just gotten the next section of pieces pinned together when the doorbell rang.

"Now what did I forget?" she grumbled as she set down the material and dragged herself across the room.

She opened the door to find Nora and the quilting group gathered on the other side.

"We aren't going to take no for an answer," Nora announced as she and the ladies marched into the apartment.

"What? How did—"

"We'll answer all your questions once we get settled," Nora said as the ladies began pulling quilting supplies from their bags.

Stunned, she was just about to close the door behind them when Ben stepped up to the threshold. "I know you didn't want any help, Molly, but we're here whether you like it or not."

14

Molly glared at Ben, hiding her surprise at his presence. "I shouldn't even let you in the door."

"Ever heard of innocent until proven guilty?"

Sure she had, but in her court of law, the evidence proved conclusive. "Still not going to 'fess up?"

"I have nothing to confess to."

The look on his face showed not one iota of guilt. His eyes were clear, if not a little hurt by her accusations. C'mon, her mind argued, how could he play innocent when she'd found the fabric in his office? Why would Ben go out of his way to help her, even kiss her senseless, then steal the one thing sure to make her hate him? And if he did take it, why would he hang around? Help her put the new quilt together? Was it guilt or subterfuge to throw her off?

"Right." She walked away before her building temper went south and she'd say something dumb like, how could you set me up for a fall? You kissed me. I thought we meant something to each other.

The ladies spread the new quilt on Molly's table, discussing strategy.

"There's no point in going any further," she announced. "Ben shouldn't have brought you here. I plan on finishing the quilt alone."

Nora eyed her. "Your stubborn streak is not very attractive."

"I've made up my mind."

"I can see that."

Nora nodded to Miss Anne, then took Molly's arm to lead her to the balcony on the other side of the sliding doors. Once outside, Nora closed the glass slider. Molly crossed her arms over her chest, a mutinous pout on her lips.

"This is very unbecoming behavior."

Molly's mouth gaped. "So is Ben's theft."

Nora sighed. "Sit."

Knowing she'd have no peace until her friend spoke her mind, Molly sat. Nora took the chair beside her. "What does Ben have to gain by taking your quilt?"

She held up the fingers of her hand as she counted down. "One, he takes away my donation from the Expo so his quilt will be front and center. Two, he messes with my magazine story. Three, he finishes the challenge successfully. Four, he gets the promotion."

"Quite a list you have there."

"It's the truth."

"You think so badly of him?"

"What? No." The question came as a surprise because deep down, she wanted him to be innocent. "I know he's ambitious."

"And has he given you any reason to suspect his behavior?"

"Yes, when he suggested the quilt you all worked on be part of the Expo."

"At the time, he thought you were making headway in the competition and thought he needed an edge."

"You see."

"But he also discussed it with me beforehand."

Molly frowned. He'd cared enough to talk to Nora first?

"It's more than that. He's seen how committed you are to Second Chances. How you give your time and resources to an organization you believe in. He wants to feel a part of something bigger."

"Sounds convenient to me," she groused, sounding infantile even to herself.

"Molly, why are you unable to see he might have nothing to do with the disappearance of your quilt. Maybe there is more here than meets the eye."

"Like what? Bottom line, he gets the promotion."

"The promotion is the only thing bothering you?"

Molly jumped up, paced a few minutes before tears threatened. "You want the real truth?" she whispered. "I thought there was something between us. A spark. Not just as colleagues." She squeezed her eyes shut, remembering his kiss, embarrassed and hurt at the same time. "At least on my part."

Nora remained silent.

"I feel like a fool. I trusted him, Nora." She opened her eyes. "Hoped we could have something beyond a work relationship."

"So you automatically assume because you have feelings for him, he would hurt you?"

She nodded.

"Oh, dear," Nora hurried to Molly's side. "He's been doing everything in his power to resolve the situation. Even though he knew you wouldn't be happy, he brought us here to help you. Pretty valiant for a man who doesn't care about you."

She shrugged, fresh out of words.

"Despite how things look, Ben is a good man."

She'd believed he was a good man before the quilt went missing, hadn't she? And if Nora was right, things hadn't changed.

"Let us help you, Molly. You can still come out ahead."

Doubtful, but then Nora always had more optimism than any person she'd ever known.

"I appreciate the help, but as I keep reminding everyone, the quilt is my project."

"And why do you insist on finishing it yourself?"

"Because of the promise I made to my readers. I don't want to blow it."

"But Molly, don't you see? You have a brand-new story now."

Molly brushed her tears away. "What are you saying?"

"If you'd take a step back and be reasonable, you'd see the real story has been more about the women who sent in the letters than the stories themselves. You say you feel a kindred spirit with these women now. Imagine how much stronger the story becomes when you write about how your friends rallied around you after the quilt went missing? You thought so highly of your readers, you allowed your friends to help you work night and day to complete another quilt. Talk about a connection. What is better than friends working beside you as the clock counts down? Don't you think many of those women would do the same thing for their friends? Wouldn't *you* be the first person to drop everything and help one of us?"

She squeezed Molly's hand.

"It's not just about you, Molly. Your premise has turned into a living entity. Once your readers learn about all the obstacles you've endured to get the special quilt issue completed, how you allowed the women in your life to aid you in your time of need, don't you think they'll be deeply touched? The moral of the story is about supporting each other. No one is an island, Molly. Having people in our lives enriches us. It's as simple as that."

Why hadn't she seen the truth? The quilt wasn't about Molly. It never had been. She'd selfishly taken on a role opposed to her original intent. The letters had been about community. She had been wrong to make the focus on *her* quilt.

Suddenly, the light bulb went on. Leave it to Nora to take all of Molly's crazy concerns and distill them down to one point. She needed her friends as much as they needed to help her right now.

Ben brought them all together for this reason. He got it, because he needed connection as much as the rest of them. The difference was, he'd started from scratch while Molly already had all the love and support she'd ever need.

"Molly, look at your life. You've always been interested in helping women. You volunteer at Second Chances for the same exact reason. Now, with a new focus on your magazine article, you're showing women there's strength in numbers. When we work together, things get done. We have each other's backs, as the young people say.

"You're always helping others, Molly. Give us the honor of helping you."

Molly smiled a sloppy grin. After such a glaring revelation, she couldn't say no. "You know it bugs me when you're always right."

"It's my age, dear. I look at things with a different perception."

"I'd say it's more like wisdom, but whatever, it works." Molly folded her friend in a hug. "Thank you," she whispered.

"No need. I'm sure you would have figured it out on your own."

Molly laughed. "I doubt it."

"Now, what are you going to do about Ben?"

"I think the question of the hour is, he got to you, didn't he?"

"Yes, dear, he did." Nora's expression turned serious. "Don't let this misunderstanding come between you two. There's more here than you'll allow yourself to see."

Maybe, but she couldn't take a chance. Not with the end of the challenge so close. She needed her guard up. After Mr. Masterson announced his decision, she'd sort out her feelings for Ben.

Nora squeezed her hand. "Give him some hope, Molly."

They went back inside to find the women, and Ben, busy stitching. He held a needle in his hand, looking clumsy, but willing to work. She didn't know what happened to the original quilt or his part in it, but she couldn't ignore the way her heart swelled as she watched him.

He didn't have to be here. Didn't have to bring the ladies here, yet he did. Could he feel more for her than she thought?

She reached for a hoop, ready to resume stitching. Listening to the lively conversation around her, she realized Ben had become part of the group. A part of their little family. Wasn't that what he'd been missing? Family? So why take a chance and lose what he'd gained by taking the quilt?

She didn't have the answers, but she did have sewing to do. Feeling Ben's gaze on her, she kept her eyes on the task at hand, not daring to look at him. Because if their gazes met, he'd know for sure, despite the circumstances, she'd lost her heart to him.

The following Monday morning, Molly's stomach twisted in knots. Today, Mr. Masterson would reveal his choice for editor-in-chief. Wasn't this going to be fun?

She entered her small office, Taylor on her heels.

"So, how's it going with the new quilt?"

"Better than I hoped for. My quilting group came over and we made lots of headway."

Taylor blew out a breath of relief. "Then we're saved for the Expo."

Molly nodded. "It's not quite like the original, but I have a better story now." She explained Nora's spin on Molly's original idea.

"I love it," Taylor gushed. "It's perfect."

"We have Nora to thank."

"Doesn't matter where it came from as long as it works." She frowned. "I still can't figure out how anyone could have walked off with the original quilt."

"You and me both." Molly noticed a pink message on her desk and picked it up to read it. "Mrs. Wilcox called?"

"Oh, yeah. Apparently something happened with the director at Second Chances. She was calling to ask if you knew anyone to fill the position. They're putting out feelers."

"Wow. I never understood why Tammi took the job in the first place when she didn't seem to like it." Molly placed the note back on her desk.

"Who knows why people do things."

"Like not tell her friend she's dating her brother?"

Taylor's cheeks went pink. "Sorry. We were testing the waters before we said anything."

She sent Taylor a reassuring smile. "Nice move. I can see you two together."

"We'll see how it goes. Once he reports back to duty, we'll have to deal with the whole long-distance thing."

"You know I'll be there any way I can."

"Yes, I do." Taylor took a breath. "You ready for the meeting?"

"What's to be ready for? Ben won."

"You don't know for sure."

"Taylor, I almost missed the kayak outing and I lost the quilt an entire magazine issue revolves around."

"Still, maybe he doesn't know."

Molly arched an amused brow. "Mr. Masterson knows everything."

Taylor's shoulders drooped. "Yeah, you're right."

"Look, I'm ready for whatever he decides. Maybe I'm not cut out for the position."

"I disagree."

"Because you're my good friend."

"No, because you're a good editor."

"Well, I'm still not getting my hopes up."

Taylor hugged her. "I'm on your side no matter what happens."

Molly swallowed around the lump in her throat.

Taylor left and Molly pulled herself together. She glanced at her watch. Thirty minutes to go. The butterflies in her stomach went on a rampage again. Taking a deep breath, she straightened up her already tidy desk, picking up the memo from Mrs. Wilcox. She stared at it a long time before picking up the phone.

Ten minutes early, Ben stood outside Masterson's office, too nervous to sit and worry. The time had come for Masterson's decision. While he should be excited, he dreaded the meeting.

If he did get the promotion, he didn't want it at Molly's expense. She'd worked hard and deserved the position as much as he did. After much soul searching, he'd come up with a way to solve both their problems and hoped Masterson would consider his idea.

The elevator dinged, revealing Molly, dressed in a pretty print dress, carrying a briefcase. To think, a month ago she'd worn what he considered her uniform of boxy suit jacket and matching skirt or slacks. In contrast, today's dress swirled around her legs when she walked. So different from the Molly who'd started this challenge with him. And she'd kept the contacts. Thank goodness for small concessions. He loved looking at her beautiful blue eyes without obstruction. She stopped in the waiting area as he rose from his chair.

"Ready?" he asked.

"To get the meeting over with."

He cringed. "I wish circumstances had played out differently."

"I messed up, Ben. I'll accept the consequences."

Before he had a chance to argue, Masterson's secretary ushered them into his office.

Compared to the meeting four weeks ago, today's meeting had more at stake for both of them, not just professionally, but personally, too. So much had changed, mainly his feelings for Molly.

He'd underestimated her as a woman. And come to appreciate her. Her work ethic rivaled his, but her heart was ten times bigger. She touched many lives, including his own.

And not only his life but his heart as well. Sometime in the four weeks, she'd inched her way into his walled-off heart and made him wonder if she could ever love him, because he wanted her love. Wanted her in his life. He'd hoped to tell her before the quilt went missing. Now he could only try to make the best of their crazy situation better for both of them.

"Have a seat," Masterson said as they filed into the room. "I promise not to keep you in suspense."

Ben waited until Molly sat down before lowering himself into the matching chair.

"We're ready whenever you are," Molly said.

Masterson rested his elbows on the desk and steepled his fingers as he regarded them both. The collar of Ben's shirt constricted his airflow, but he didn't dare tug at it.

"I have to say, the challenge idea turned out better than I had anticipated. Both of you showed me what the position and Master's Publishing mean to you."

Ben shifted, sending a quick glance Molly's way. She stared straight ahead.

"Ben, you completed the challenge. The quilt is finished and registered with the Expo for auction, and you kept the day-to-day running of *Outdoor Life* on track. I'm impressed."

"Thank you."

"Molly." Masterson shook his head. "You turned out to be quite the surprise."

"In a good or bad way?"

Masterson chuckled. "I knew you had spirit, you just needed a fire lit under you. Once that happened, you showed me how committed you are to the company."

When she opened her mouth to speak, Masterson held up his hand to stop her. "You've been a loyal employee. I had no doubt you'd take this challenge and run with it. Things were going quite well until Saturday."

"I don't mean to make excuses, but I had a good reason for arriving late."

"Yes, the missing quilt." He frowned. "I have to say, I don't like the turn of events. Any luck finding it?"

"No, sir. But I've been able to put another quilt together to be featured at the Expo."

He raised a brow. "So fast?"

She glanced at Ben. "I had help."

Masterson glanced between them. "Is it true, Ben?"

"Yes, sir. I made sure Molly had all the help she needed to get back on track."

"Even though she thinks you were behind the theft?"

Molly gaped at their boss.

Ben crossed his arms over his chest.

"Office gossip does make it up here, but rest assured, I never believed you would stoop so low. The fact you recruited everyone in the office, as well as the entire building, to search for the quilt proves you want a resolution to the issue, not because you created the problem."

Turning to face Ben, Molly's eyes shimmered. "I didn't know."

"I told you, Molly, I had nothing to do with the quilt going missing."

"It's a mystery, but not the reason you two are here." Masterson rose from his desk, sauntering to the side credenza to pour a glass of water into a cut crystal glass. He took a drink, then returned.

Ben's heart did another round of calisthenics. He knew Masterson loved the dramatic, but his delaying tactics bordered on ridiculous.

"When I issued the challenge, I wanted to see how well you would work under pressure. Ben, you're new to the company and I hadn't had a chance to see you function under stress. Molly, you've been here a long time but have never lived up to the potential I believe you to have. Before making my decision, I had to get you both out of your comfort zones. I think I accomplished the feat quite well."

He folded his hands on top of the desk.

"*American Legend* is going to be a magazine filled with passion about deserving people. I must say, it has taken hold of my interest like no other magazine I've developed. I need the best to make it run efficiently and profitably."

He took another sip of water.

"After Saturday, I thought for sure Ben would come out the winner. Until I learned you both worked together to make a new quilt. You both have the heart I need to run my magazine, therefore putting me in a difficult position. I want you both."

Ben exchanged a surprised glance with Molly, then back to Masterson. "Before you go on sir, may I speak?"

Masterson nodded.

"I agree with your assessment about Molly and me. Working as a team." He shot a quick glance at Molly. "We do work well together."

He took a deep breath. Time to put it out there. "I'd like to ask you to consider making us coeditors. I believe together we can take the magazine to the next level and beyond."

Molly's eyes went wide with surprise. "Oh, Ben . . . I don't think—"

He stopped her. "I had to put the idea out there, Molly."

She looked away and his heart sank.

Masterson regarded him for a long time, drawing out the moment. "Interesting proposal, Ben. I can see you've put much thought into your suggestion."

"Yes, sir. I have."

"Hmm. Now you've put me in a quandary."

Masterson went quiet again. Ben could almost imagine the wheels turning in his brilliant mind.

"Putting your idea aside for a moment, Ben, I have to say I'm impressed with Molly's fortitude, and I can't overlook her initiative. Instead of accepting defeat, you did make the kayak challenge and managed to put together a new quilt. You see, Molly's attitude is the heart and soul of *American Legend*. The type of dedication I need from the individual I've selected as editor-in-chief."

Ben watched as Molly blinked, stunned by the announcement. "Are you saying I got the job?"

"Yes, Molly. Despite Ben's proposal, I choose you."

Ben couldn't ignore the disappointment heavy in his chest, but he'd decided last night even if Masterson shot down his idea and gave Molly the position, he'd keep working hard to get the next promotion. He wasn't going anywhere. Especially since he had to convince Molly they were a chance worth taking.

Molly placed her hand over her heart. "I don't know what to say."

"How about, when do I start?"

"I'm afraid I can't."

Masterson's smiled dimmed. "Excuse me?"

She opened her briefcase and reached inside, removing an envelope. Ben's stomach sank as she slid it across Masterson's desk. "I can't accept the position."

He'd wondered why she bothered bringing a briefcase to the meeting. Now he understood.

Masterson placed his fingertips on the edge of the envelope and dragged it toward him. "And this is?"

"My resignation."

"Molly, I just gave you a promotion. I can see why you might have thought you lost the challenge, well, because you did, but I want you for the job."

"Mr. Masterson, I learned a lot during the challenge. I did want the position. And if you had told me yesterday I'd gotten it, I would have been beyond thrilled."

"Then what happened?" Ben asked, stunned she would give up the prize she'd worked so hard to attain.

She turned in the chair to face him. "I've come to understand I want to make a difference in the world. And while Mr. Masterson's plan is to have the new magazine touch people's lives with inspiring stories and personal testimonies, I want to *live* these stories. I can't do that in an office, tucked away from people. I need to be working every day with those who need what I can give them."

She turned back to Masterson. "I've decided to take the position of director at Second Chances. I'm needed there." She sent a sideways glance at Ben. "And here, Ben will make an awesome editor-in-chief. If the offer still stands."

Ruffled, Masterson said, "Yes. Of course."

Ben's chest constricted from the bittersweet news of Molly's departure and the fact he did get the job after all.

Molly stood, smoothing her dress. "I've given you two weeks' notice. I suggest Taylor as my replacement. She knows the ins and outs of the magazine, and she is very good at her job. I can transition her, or whoever you name as my replacement, before I leave."

Masterson leaned back in his chair. "Is there anything I can do to change your mind?"

"I'm afraid not. I've made my decision."

"All right then." He glanced at Ben. "Congratulations on your promotion."

Ben stood. "Thank you, sir."

"I have to say, you've thrown me off, Molly, and that rarely happens. I need to regroup." He waved them off. "Ben, we'll discuss the particulars later."

Ben followed Molly from the office as they made their way to the elevator. After he pushed the button, he asked, "Why?"

"It's like I said back in the office. The challenge shook me out of my comfort zone. Going head to head with you proved I can go after any goal I put my mind to. And what I want is to make a difference in people's lives."

The doors opened and they stepped inside.

"My time here at the magazine has been wonderful, but it's time to move on. I'm excited about the possibilities, Ben. About what I can accomplish for the women who need more than they can hope for in their lives."

How could he argue? "You're positive then?"

She laid a hand on his arm. The tender gesture added pressure to his already-tight chest. "I'm positive. And you'll make an awesome editor-in-chief. It's what you've wanted all along. With you at the helm, the magazine will be a success. Win-win all around."

Maybe professionally, but what about keeping Molly in his life? "Listen, Molly, I—"

She stopped him before he could tell her what she meant to him, and explain while he was thankful for her support, he needed her in his life.

"You're welcome."

The door swished open on their floor. His time with Molly cut short.

Before stepping out her gaze roamed the elevator and she grinned. "I'm going to miss our little elevator chats."

"Molly—" He tried to explain again, but before he could, Taylor ran over and swept Molly away. He curled his hands into tight fists. Where was his usual confidence when he needed it?

Hovering between disappointment and astonishment over the way he'd gotten the promotion, he strode back to his office. He might have gotten the promotion today, but he still had work to do.

"Way to go," Charlie said as he met him at the door. "You got it."

"By default," Ben said as he made his made his way to the desk.

"Who cares how you got it?" Charlie high-fived him. "I knew we'd win."

"We? When did this become a team effort?"

"C'mon. You couldn't have won without my help."

"I didn't need your help. If Molly hadn't resigned, I'd still be editor here."

Charlie frowned, perplexed. "Yeah, who would have figured? All the work messing up her chances and she resigns anyway."

A sinking sensation settled in Ben's gut. "What did you do, Charlie?"

Realizing what he'd just admitted, Charlie's gaze shifted. "Just shifted the odds in your favor."

Ben rounded the desk. "You took the quilt?"

Charlie shot him a smug grin. "Sure."

So taken aback, for a few seconds Ben couldn't come up with any words.

"You know," Charlie went on to explain. "She was an easy target from the start. Getting her involved on the kayak trip with those troubled kids worked in our favor. She can't resist a cause."

Ben's temper started heating up. "She did quite well."

"She surprised everyone. Including you. There was the problem. You stopped looking at her as an easy mark."

"Your point?"

"When she starting gaining on you, I came up with the idea to take the quilt. Figured it would mess her up on so many levels she'd never recover."

"Except her recovery is the exact reason she got the job. If you hadn't interfered, I would have been Masterson's first choice."

"Yeah," Charlie grumbled. "There is that."

Ben ran a hand through his hair. "How did you do it?"

"It was easy. I kept an eye on her office. When she went for coffee, I snuck in with a garbage bag, snatched it and ran. I emptied a few trash bins in the main office, just to throw off suspicion. No one even noticed."

"I can't believe it." Ben shoved his hands in his pants pockets, so he wouldn't shake the man wearing the glib expression. "She blamed me."

"And it worked, too." Charlie cut his hand through the air. "Could you see? She was getting to you, man. I could see it. You two had this . . . thing going. Everyone in the office noticed it. I had to put a stop to it before you lost your mind."

It wasn't his mind he'd lost. It was his heart.

"So you put some of the fabric in my office to make me look guilty?"

"I had to make it legit, so you two would be at odds." He grinned again. "Worked."

Yes, it did. Too well. But maybe the whole sordid event could be salvaged. "Where is the quilt now?"

"I gave it to the janitor and asked him to stash it in the supply closet on the main floor until I could get rid of it. I figured I'd have to wait a few weeks until things die down."

It was all Ben could do to keep from grabbing Charlie's collar. "Do you have any idea how much work went into the quilt?"

"Chill, man. Who cares? You won."

"No, I didn't."

In more ways than one. He'd lost any hope of being with Molly because of Charlie's actions. Unless he made things right.

He lit out of the office, poking at the elevator button until the doors opened. Once on the main level, he found the janitorial closet. Locked. Frustrated, he kicked the door, then ran to the security desk at the main entrance, convincing the security guard to unlock the closet door.

Breathing a prayer, he entered, hoping beyond hope to find the quilt still stashed there. He went through every shelf, but no garbage bag. Leaning back against the door, discouraged and angry, he scanned the closet one final time. On the top of a shelf, stuffed back almost out of sight, he noticed a black plastic bag.

"Please be the quilt."

Grabbing a nearby stool, he scrambled up and snatched the edge of the bag to pull it toward him. Once the bag fell into his arms, he tugged it open. His heart skipped a beat.

Inside he found the crumpled Hearts Entwined quilt.

⁂

Ben leaned against the doorjamb of Molly's office, a self-satisfied smile on his lips. Now what did the man want? She'd tried to brush him off earlier, after the meeting with Mr. Masterson, so it wouldn't be so hard to say good-bye. It seemed Ben wasn't going to make her leaving any easier than it had to be.

"I'm usually not one to say I told you so, but in this case, I'm gonna say it."

She sat back in her chair. "Entertain me."

He pushed off and stepped into her office, pulling a large bag he'd kept hidden on the other side of the door. With flare, he flipped it onto her desk.

"You're bringing me garbage?"

"Open it."

"Then will you go away?"

He went serious. "If you want me to."

199

No, she didn't want him to. How silly of her after everything that had happened. Curious, she stood, pulled the plastic strings, and peered inside. Gasped when she saw the quilt inside.

"I told you so."

Hot tears blurred her sight as Molly reached in and removed the quilt. She hugged it to her first before spreading it on her work-table, checking it over inch by inch. "How on earth did you find it?"

Ben walked up beside her. "Charlie took it. He thought it would give me an advantage in winning the challenge."

"But why would he do such a thing?"

"Because if I moved upstairs, he got my office."

"Explains a lot." She ran her fingers over the soft material. "But not what happened in Mr. Masterson's office. Why did you want us to work together?"

"During these past weeks, I realized we work well together. I thought if I could convince Masterson to make us coeditors, it took the pressure off both of us. We'd both get what we wanted." He reached out to take her hand from the quilt and entwine his fingers with hers. "I didn't want us to be rivals any longer."

The tightness in her chest eased some as she saw the truth in his eyes. "You were willing to sacrifice your ambitions to share the position with me?"

"It's what you do when you're crazy in love with someone."

She placed her free hand on his chest, directly over the heart of the man she'd falsely accused. The man she'd fallen hopelessly in love with. Tears welled in her eyes. "Ben, I am so sorry I accused you."

"You should have known better. I'd never do anything to hurt you."

He hadn't just spoken the words. He'd proved himself to her.

"You're right. I should have known better." She blinked. "Can you ever forgive me?"

He thumbed away the tear on her cheek. "Depends."

"On?"

"Whether you'll take a chance on me. On us."

She moved both hands to cup his face, brushing her lips over his. "With a challenge like that, how can I refuse?"

Epilogue

W hy are you in such a hurry?"

Keeping her hand tucked in his, Ben led her to his secret destination. "I have a wedding present for you."

"Aren't you getting ahead of yourself?"

"Sorry. I get impatient when I want something."

Didn't she know it. But what he had was a fiancée who couldn't book a wedding into her busy schedule. As much as she'd tried, Molly couldn't settle on a date. Spring? Fall? Being engaged was new, and until she knew exactly what she wanted for their wedding, she would wait.

So much had changed in a short time. Molly had set up an office at Second Chances, full of fresh ideas to help the women who walked through the doors of the renovated center. Ben had moved to the upstairs office at Master's Publishing, starting work on the debut issue of *American Legend*. Taylor had taken over Molly's job, excited to be promoted to editor. Charlie had been fired. Mr. Masterson made it clear he didn't want anyone lacking integrity working for him.

Ben led her through the busy aisles of the Charity Expo, stopping by the main quilt display. Set up in a corner of the room, Molly's quilt, the original one, was mounted and displayed as one of the items up for auction. Next to it, also mounted, was the quilt Ben and the ladies had worked on as part of the challenge. On a plaque, between the two pieces, a sign Mr. Masterson had added to boost publicity read, "Rival Hearts. Courtesy of Master's Publishing."

Molly chuckled. You'd think the man was responsible for matchmaking. But his tactics worked. Once word had spread about the outcome of the challenge, and how Ben had saved the day by finding the quilt, interest for both quilts had doubled.

"There you are, my two favorite people," Sarah Lowery, the woman behind the Expo, gushed as she joined them. "I can't believe the strings your publisher pulled to make today's turnout the best we've ever had."

"It's what he does," Ben quipped, looking antsy. Molly could tell he wanted to move on to their real destination.

"You'll both be present when we auction the quilts, right? Your added presence will encourage the bidders."

"We promised, Sarah. We'll be here."

"Thank you," she said, her smile bright. "Thank you so very much."

Sarah turned on her heel and moved back into the crowd, greeting attendees like they were long-lost family.

"Let's go." Ben tugged her again as they made their way to the other side of the room. He stopped beside a table filled with projects completed by Nora and the quilting group. Nora and Miss Anne manned the table.

"I haven't seen you all morning," Nora admonished with glee. "Since Ben's claimed you for his own, we rarely see you."

Molly smiled at Ben. "It's only been a week."

Once they admitted their love, he'd gone down on one knee and popped the question. She knew beyond a shadow of a doubt she loved Ben. She didn't have to take her time saying yes.

Miss Anne winked. "I remember those days of young love."

Ben rounded the table. "Where is it?"

"I put it in a safe place," Nora told him as she pulled a large box from beneath the table. She handed it over to Ben. A smile curved his lips.

How had she gotten so lucky? After all they'd been through, they'd been blessed with a love Molly never thought she'd find. The love of a good man who made her heart race and her dreams come true. He supported her move to Second Chances. Encouraged her to go after her goals and ambitions.

He walked back to Molly and handed her the box. "Go ahead. Open it."

"So this is the big surprise, huh? When did you have time to buy it?"

"When you stopped to talk business with Mrs. Wilcox. I knew once the two of you got talking about the center, I'd have plenty of time to make my purchase and get back to you."

"You didn't have to get me anything."

"Consider it an engagement present."

Heart full of joy, Molly opened the box. She pulled back the white tissue paper to find a quilt folded neatly inside. She set the box on the table and unfolded the quilt, her brows raised in surprise.

"The second heart quilt?"

"Yep. But I had it customized."

"It's not a car." She snorted. "You can't customize a quilt."

"Sure you can." He winked at Nora. "When you have help."

Once the original quilt had been located and returned, Nora asked Molly if she could hold onto the second quilt they had worked on as a team. So busy with work changes and her new relationship with Ben, she hadn't given it a second thought.

"Look here." Ben spread it out and pointed to the middle section where the two hearts met. The original fabric had been replaced. The pink piece, Molly recognized from her blanket. A new section of red with tiny baseballs, bats, and mitts, had been added.

Molly traced the two pieces. "Yours?"

"From when I was a kid." He wrapped his arm around her shoulder. "I gave it to Nora and she added it. And if you look closely, you'll see our initials embroidered together."

Blinking back tears of happiness, which now seemed to sneak up on a regular basis, she smiled at Ben. "You didn't have to," she repeated.

Ben smiled at Molly, his arm squeezing her close. "Of course I did. It'll be proof to show our grandkids someday."

Yes, proof even two rivals could fall in love and have their own happily ever after.

Discussion Questions

1. In the beginning of the book, it took a challenge from her boss to make Molly realize she wanted more out of life. Have you ever needed a push to get what you want out of life? What incident caused a positive change in you?

2. Sometimes we fail to see the hand of God in certain situations in our lives. What are some ways we could be more aware of Him working for our good?

3. When Molly explained why the quilt she would feature in her magazine meant so much to her, could you relate?

4. Ben thought he had the challenge won before it started. What happened to make him think he might be in trouble?

5. Community is important in our lives, whether in friends, family, or church. How did each of these fit into Molly's life?

6. Once the challenge got underway, Molly began to look at herself differently. In what ways did she do this? Does your Christian walk challenge you to see yourself differently?

7. Ben thought all he wanted was a place to settle down. How did his expectations change as the story progressed?

8. Molly's desire to help other women never wavered in the story. Where do you think this passion came from?

9. When Molly thought the quilt was gone for good she was heartbroken, but her friends showed her all was not lost. What did Nora say to get Molly to look at the situation in a different light?

10. While both Molly and Ben wanted the new job, they needed love more. What did they learn about themselves and each other?

Want to learn more about author
Tara Randel and check out other great
fiction from Abingdon Press?

Sign up for our fiction newsletter at
www.AbingdonPress.com
to read interviews with your favorite authors, find tips
for starting a reading group, and stay posted on what
new titles are on the horizon. It's a place to connect
with other fiction readers or post a
comment about this book.

Be sure to visit Tara online!

www.tararandel.com

And now for a sneak peek at

A Grand Design
by Amber Stockton

From the new Quilts of Love Series.

∞

1

I hate the month of June!"

Alyssa Denham shouldered her way through the revolving door to her office building and onto the concrete sidewalk, her arms laden with bridal shower grab-bag gifts. She should have tossed most of the stuff, or found an unsuspecting coworker and bestowed the gifts on her as a random act of kindness. Three office bridal showers in the first three weeks of April. It had to be a record. The predictable wedding invitations arrived in her inbox, and she still didn't have a date for the events. Some of it was her fault. It shouldn't bother her, but it did.

I don't have a date, period.

Every year for the past five years, whenever a wedding occurred for someone she knew, it happened in June. And this year was no different. If June was her least favorite month, then April followed as a close second. As Alyssa stepped out from under the overhang, the light drizzle falling most of the day had become a steady rain.

"Perfect," she muttered, looking up and down the street for a taxi to the train station. She usually walked, but the gift bags and little wrapped items she carried made the idea impossible. The six blocks would feel more like sixty.

Alyssa straightened when she saw a yellow cab round the corner. She stepped forward and tried to free one arm to signal it. When the driver maneuvered toward the curb, relief coursed through her. Just as she reached for the door handle, a Tom Cruise look-alike in a dark gray tailored suit stepped in front of her. He opened the door and held it for a young blonde who could easily pass for a magazine model.

Recognizing the girl as the latest bride-to-be from her office, Alyssa rolled her eyes and sighed. The pretty girls always get the guys—and the cabs. So what if the girl was also in a jam. The young woman and her fiancé might be late for dinner reservations, but Alyssa had an armful of packages—thanks to the two who had just stolen her ride. The cab pulled away from the curb and the rear wheels sent a spray of water in her direction.

Her favorite cream slacks now sporting a dirty rainwater splatter, Alyssa headed for the corner to catch the city bus. It arrived just as she reached the stop. Balancing her bags on one arm, she managed to withdraw enough loose change from the purse dangling on her arm for the fare, then turned to find a seat. Sandwiched between a woman in a black business suit and stiletto heels with a cell phone pressed to her ear and a fifty-something gentleman with a rounded middle and gray-speckled hair, Alyssa couldn't wait to get home.

If you don't do something besides work and stay at home, you'll never meet Mr. Right. Live a little, Alyssa!

The admonishment from her best friend floated through her mind as she surveyed the other riders. From the shabbily-dressed, college-age crowd to the handful of silver-haired men headed for retirement, there wasn't a prospect in the bunch—unless she counted the Don Juan type with the slicked-back hair and gold-capped smile who eyed her from across the aisle. At only twenty-nine, she wasn't that desperate yet.

Well, Lord, I would live a little. But on my salary, this is about as social as it gets.

Thankfully, the ride to the train station wasn't long, and Alyssa stepped off the bus. Grateful to be under shelter, she smiled and thanked the man who held the door for her and headed inside to catch her train.

Forty minutes later, she walked through the door to her comfortable two-bedroom apartment. She deposited her armload onto the maple dining room table her grandmother had given her and breathed a sigh of relief. Alyssa flipped through the stack of mail. Nothing but bills and advertisements. She sighed. The usual. Suddenly, a bold word on the front of one envelope caught her attention.

WINNER!

Alyssa stared at the return address. Oh, no! How in the world had this happened? She'd entered the magazine contest on a dare. And now, she'd won? She'd never won anything before in her life. Was this God's answer to her current solitary life, or was He pulling her leg? Alyssa smiled. It had to be a God-thing.

But why this? And why Mackinac Island of all places?

Curious, Alyssa slit the envelope and pulled out the full-color, tri-fold brochure along with a letter. She kicked off her pumps, padded over to her favorite burgundy recliner, and extended the footrest. The one lone accent piece in her otherwise neutral décor. Settled into the cozy comfort of the soft velour, Alyssa scanned the enticing images and well-written descriptions. Just the way the mind of her youth remembered it. As if nothing had changed in all these years. The image of a lighthouse and a few seagulls reminded her of her father and the walks they used to take along the beach. Speculating on the types of people who had walked the beach leaving prints behind had been a favorite pastime for both of them.

Every written description in the brochure promised an unforgettable time. And each picture included a happy couple enjoying the boating activities, horseback riding, rafting, and tennis, not to mention the horse-drawn carriage rides and scrumptious dinner selections. She'd done it all at one point many years ago. Advertising the island as a romantic getaway made sense. But it didn't make her current status any easier to swallow.

Couples, couples, couples! Didn't singles go anywhere anymore? Just once she'd like to see a vacation spot showing someone having a grand old time alone. But as she unfolded the brochure, each new page revealed another toothy twosome, caught up in euphoric delight. And she was a onesome—an unsmiling onesome. Blotting out the images of the couples, she focused on the swimming, boating, and nature walks—things she loved to do and hadn't done since she was a kid. And she hadn't taken her vacation yet this year. Why not throw out the romance and do a getaway for one?

But just the thought of going alone dampened her excitement. She'd played the odd-woman-out too many times. Not her idea of fun. She stared at the word *two* in the letter as if it were a death sentence. Two. Then, a flash of enlightenment tugged at the corners of her mouth. Not a couple. Just two.

Alyssa snapped the recliner into its upright position and reached for the phone on the end table next to the chair. After dialing, she waited for her best friend to pick up. One . . . two . . .

Alyssa straightened as the third ring stopped midway through and planted her feet on the carpeted floor. "Libby, you'll never guess what's happened."

"What?" Libby's excitement transcended the distance between them.

"Remember the contest the girls dared me to enter in the latest *Bride* magazine?" Alyssa twirled the phone cord around her fingers and leaned back. "Where I wrote the short paragraph about why

I needed a vacation? The one promising a chance to win an all-expense paid trip for two and touted it as a 'honeymoon in heaven'?"

"How could I forget? You almost wouldn't complete the thing," Libby complained. "And I had to dare you to mail it." Her friend's breath hitched. "Wait, don't tell me."

"Yep. I have the notification right here in my hand." Alyssa held the phone away to avoid being deafened by Libby's shriek. "There's only one snag," she said when it was safe. Tucking a strand of her cinnamon-colored hair behind her ear, she pivoted and propped her feet on the edge of the end table. "The getaway is for two."

"Now you listen to me, Alyssa Denham . . ." Libby predictably launched into attack mode. "It is not a problem. We'll figure something out. I mean, you are always looking for some excuse to get out of changing your dull routine. If you can find any reason whatsoever not to do something, you will use it. This is just the kind of thing—"

"I want you to come with me," Alyssa interrupted, grinning.

"—you do all the time. And frankly, I'm . . ." Silence filled the line, followed by an incredulous, "What?"

Alyssa smiled. "I said I'm going, and I want you to go with me."

"All right. Who are you? And what have you done with my best friend? Alyssa would not agree to do something like this so easily."

Alyssa laughed. "It's me, Libby."

"Well, you sure don't sound like the Alyssa I know and love. She would die before she'd make up her mind this quickly. I mean, this is the girl who waited a year before getting her hair cut in the latest style. She got her ears pierced ten years after all her friends did. And she waits until styles go out of season before she decides she likes them enough to buy them. So this can't be Alyssa."

Alyssa crossed her ankles and picked imaginary lint off her cable-knit sweater. "Well, God and I had a little chat about my life on the bus ride home. And when I walked in the door, this letter was waiting. Seemed like a quick answer to me, so I decided to go." Glancing back at the brochure on her lap, Alyssa sighed. "Just maybe, the friend you know is changing. Maybe she's looking for a little excitement in her life."

"Wow. I always said it would take an act of God to get you to break out of the rut you call a life, but who knew He'd take me seriously."

Alyssa shook her head. Leave it to Libby to be sarcastic. They'd been best friends for almost twenty years. Libby's rather boisterous style and brand of wit is what attracted Alyssa. Inwardly, she hoped some of it would rub off on her.

"Come on, Libby. Cut me some slack here. You're the one who's always telling me to live a little. So are you in or out? Answer quickly before I have time to talk myself out of it."

"In," Libby exclaimed. "Just bear with me. I'm still in shock." She paused and took a breath. "And it's free? No catches, no time-share spiels to listen to?"

Alyssa picked up the letter of confirmation, reading it again, barely believing it herself. "It says so right here. I have the letter here to prove it." She reclined the chair back and stared at the stucco finish on the ceiling, the white speckled design resembling the intricate patterns on the sand-washed rocks she had on the shelf in her bathroom. Another reminder of the life she'd lived as a child.

"You seriously want me to come along?"

"Well, who else would I take? I don't exactly have a long line of suitors waiting at my door."

Libby's grin came through the phone line. "No, I mean wouldn't you want to take this trip alone? You never know. Mr. Right could be waiting for you. Speaking of which, where is this place?"

"Mackinac Island in Lake Huron." Alyssa examined the brochure again. "There's even something here about it being named 'Turtle Island' by the local Chippewa Indians who discovered it."

"Turtle Island?" Incredulity laced Libby's words.

Alyssa shrugged. "Hey, I don't write the descriptions." She read further. "Anyway, the brochure says it's a great getaway with lots to do and the perfect place for some excitement." Raising one eyebrow, she pursed her lips. "Somehow, I think the 'excitement' they promise has more to do with their billing this island as a romantic getaway than the kind of adventure you and I could have."

"Do tell."

"There's boating, horseback riding, cycling, parasailing—"

"Parasailing?" Libby latched onto the word. "I can see it now. A skimpy little number with a drop-dead gorgeous instructor standing behind me as I fumble with the sail and play the dimwitted damsel who can't tell which end is up."

Alyssa laughed and shook her head. Her friend's flare for the extreme is what made their friendship work. "And what if the instructor's a woman?"

"Then I'll give her to you while I scout out the *Baywatch* guy."

"Gee, thanks. Some friend you are."

"You know you love me."

"Only the Lord knows why." But Alyssa did know.

Life was an adventure to Libby, and she wanted her best friend to take part in it. Libby usually managed to pull her from her staid and simple existence to create memories far exceeding her wildest imagination.

"So other than the obvious, tell me a little more about this place."

A big ball of fur jumped up into Alyssa's lap. She waited for Kalani to find a comfortable position, then stroked the dark gray Persian's ears, earning a rumbling purr in response. "The brochure says the main hotel was built around the turn of the century, and they don't allow cars on the island."

"No cars? How do you get around?"

"Bicycles, horse-drawn carriages, and your own two legs."

"Sounds like your kind of place. No modern conveniences." Sarcasm dripped from Libby's words. "Wonder if they have indoor plumbing."

Alyssa planted her fist on one hip, startling Kalani. "I appreciate my modernized lifestyle, thank you so much." She gently coaxed the cat to relax. "But, I admit, a part of me would like to get a feel for a bygone era."

"Looks like you'll get your chance." Libby made a sound like snapping her fingers. "Hey, wait a second. Doesn't your grandmother live on the island? And isn't it the same island where you used to spend all your summers as a kid?"

"I was wondering if you'd actually remember."

"How could I forget? It was all you used to talk about when we first met. I remember wishing I could go with you just once."

"It looks like you'll get your wish," Alyssa replied, throwing her friend's words back at her.

"Guess so." She paused. "It's been a while for you, hasn't it?" came the soft words.

Libby knew all about what had happened.

Though her friend couldn't see her, Alyssa nodded. "Nearly fifteen years." Even now, moisture gathered in her eyes. She blinked several times and looked toward the ceiling. No. She wouldn't cry. She wouldn't. She couldn't. It would spoil the elation she should be feeling.

"It's been a long time."

"Yes." Alyssa snatched a tissue from the box next to her and held it to the corners of her eyes. "In some ways, it feels like yesterday. In others, like forever."

"Well, experiences and memories don't just go away. You and your dad had a lot of fun there for a lot of years."

Alyssa sniffed. "And then Dad got sick, and well, somehow the joys of going didn't hold as much enticement anymore."

"Because your mom never cared for the island. Though I'm not sure why."

"Like you, she preferred the more modern conveniences and easy access to an abundance of stores, outlets, and entertainment options." Alyssa shrugged. "The island just didn't suit her as well as it did Dad and me."

"Probably the lack of cars," Libby intoned. "Still, I think it's been far too long for you, and it's high time you returned. Guess God had the same idea."

Obviously He did. "Well, we've talked about taking a vacation together. And you said you had two weeks coming to you. I can take off as well. It's the perfect opportunity."

"When are we supposed to fly off to our land of adventure?"

Alyssa reached for the letter and scanned the page. "Umm, July seventh." She kicked her feet against the table and swung the chair around, squinting to see the calendar on the wall behind her desk in the corner. "It's a Monday."

Libby rustled some paper. "It gives us a little more than two months to plan. We can have an amazing two weeks, stop in and visit your grandmother, and get into all sorts of trouble. I can't believe this is happening."

"Me, either." Alyssa was almost tempted to pinch herself. She'd wanted a change for a while. This was just the opportunity to help her make it. And it followed all those weddings she'd been invited to attend. After being present to witness three more women she knew being joined in eternal wedded bliss, she'd need a vacation. Winning this trip sealed the deal. "We'll have a blast, whether Prince Charming is there or not."

"You're on, girlfriend," Libby chimed in, obviously infected by Alyssa's enthusiasm. "Mackinac Island, here we come!"

Well, almost. Alyssa had another phone call to make.

❧

"Oh, Alyssa dear, are you really coming back to our island?"

"Yes, Grandma, I am."

"Praise be to Jesus. My little girl is coming home." Her sniffle was like a knife in Alyssa's gut. "Oh, how I have prayed and prayed for this day to come. I'd almost given up hoping you'd ever return, dear."

"I know, Grandma, and I'm sorry." She shouldn't have stayed away so long. But the days had become weeks, and the weeks had become months, and the months had become years, and before she knew it, fifteen years had passed. "I should have made more of an effort to come see you. What with school, and my summer jobs, and planning for college, then a career, it's hard to imagine it's been as long as it has."

"Child, there is no need to apologize, though I certainly do forgive you. Your mama needed you after my Richard passed away. It isn't easy losing your soul mate, the love of your life."

Grandma knew it all too well, even if Alyssa could only imagine. First, Grandpa, and then five years later, Dad. And Alyssa had stopped her annual visits, only keeping in touch through cards or the occasional phone call.

"No." Alyssa sighed. "But it wasn't fair to you to be left all alone up there. I mean it wasn't just us. You lost Dad, too."

"Oh, child, I'm never alone on this little island. You should know. I've lived here all my life and made a lot of friends over the years." The faint sound of *Wheel of Fortune* came through the phone. One of Grandma's favorite TV programs. Hers, too. "Then, there are all the tourists. Some of them provide a great deal of entertainment for me, and I only have to watch or listen to them for ten minutes or so. Now, you stop the line of thought leading you down a path of guilt right this instant, young lady."

Alyssa could almost see Grandma wagging a finger in her direction. She straightened, as if Grandma could see her and would tell her to stop slouching in the next breath. "Yes, ma'am," she replied.

"I am doing just fine, I assure you, my dear." Her voice held all the conviction needed to make Alyssa believe it. "But to tell you the truth, your call and announcement couldn't have come at a better time."

"Oh?" Just how orchestrated *was* this trip? "What's happening?"

"Tell me again, how long is this little vacation going to be?"

"Two weeks," Alyssa replied. "Why?"

"And dear Libby is going to be joining you?"

"Yes." She sighed. "Grandma, what's all this about?"

"I have a little project for you while you're here."

"A project?" It sounded ominous. Even though Grandma couldn't see her, she narrowed her eyes and scrunched up her brows. "What kind of project?"

"Oh, just a little something to keep you busy in the midst of all the parasailing, horseback riding, and boating I know you just *love* to do."

Yeah, right. Alyssa loved all of the adrenaline-inducing activity most of the tourists sought out as much as she loved the thought of going to three weddings as a solo act. Libby might live for it, but not her. Not in this lifetime. "Now, Grandma, you know me better."

"Yes, child, I do. And it's why I know you'll be excited to learn of a little something I've been meaning to do for over a year now, but I simply haven't had the opportunity, or the ability."

Why was Grandma being so mysterious? Why not just come right out and say what she wanted Alyssa to do? It's not like she'd have any say in the matter, not where Grandma was concerned. As sweet as she was, Grandma usually managed to persuade everyone to do her bidding and make them think it was their idea in the first place.

"And I suppose Libby and I coming will now give you the opportunity?"

"Yes, dear, it will. You see, I've started a special quilt. One to unite the decades and bring together many different families. But I can't do it alone. It's going to take you and Libby helping me to make it work."

A quilt? Alyssa swallowed. As in pieces of fabric sewn together in some semblance of a pattern? Her throat constricted. She didn't know anything about quilting. She could barely sew on a button, much less attempt to make something as big as a quilt actually look good.

"Um, Grandma?" She swallowed again. "Are you certain you want me helping with this? I mean, are you sure I won't ruin whatever work you've already begun?"

"Oh, pish-posh, Alyssa dear." She could just see Grandma's hand waving off her concerns. "I know your skillset doesn't exactly involve the fine art of sewing. You leave that part to me." A chuckle. "Though I can't promise I won't attempt to teach you a little while you're here." The background sounds of the TV muted. "No, what I have in mind for you and Libby is to help me collect the various blocks to make up the larger quilt. My old body doesn't get around as easy as it once did, and your strong legs will take you all around the island."

"So, we're going to be collecting quilt blocks from other people?"

"Yes. From each lady who was once part of my quilting circle. I've lost touch with two or three of them, so reaching them might not be so easy. And two have since passed on, but their daughters or sons still live here on the island."

Oh, Libby was going to love it. It had adventure and challenge written all over it. Just the sort of thing to make Libby's day.

"You met most of them when you were a girl," Grandma continued. "So, I'm sure it won't take up much of your time. But it will mean a great deal to me to have your help."

"Of course, Grandma. You can count on Libby and me. We'd be glad to help you."

What sounded like a hand slapping a table came through the phone. "Splendid! I shall begin preparing the list of ladies' names and addresses to the best of my knowledge, and it will be ready when you arrive." She paused. "And Alyssa, dear?"

"Yes, Grandma?"

"I am pleased to know you're coming for a visit, more so than seeing this project finished. You know I do, don't you, dear?"

"Of course, Grandma." How could she doubt her?

"Very good. We shall be seeing each other soon. Between now and then, you make sure you pack your prettiest clothes and get a fresh haircut. There are quite a few handsome gentlemen on this island, and you never know who you might meet."

Alyssa rolled her eyes. First Libby, and now her grandmother. Was everyone going to try to pair her up? Libby and Grandma were both single, too. Besides, she wasn't taking this vacation to meet men. Not even to meet one man. Now, she just had to convince everyone else of it.